Tell me you love me

By. Tessa J

Tell Me You Love Me

Published by Tyanna Presents
www.tyannapresents1@gmail.com

DEDICATIONS

To my babe loving you is easy and hard at the same time. With you I learn to have patience. With you I learn to forgive. For you I understand that the journey we embark on is not always easy, but I promise it will never be a dull moment.

ACKNOWLEDGEMENTS

I'm sorry I haven't released a book in forever and to tell you truth, I was thinking about walking away from this industry for good. Not only is it messy and full of snakes it is full of people praying for your downfall. I allowed certain editors, authors, and friends to play on my confidence and say my stories didn't make sense because they didn't understand. I doubted myself instead of trusting myself and my craft. I found hidden treasures also, and they are the reason I will continue to keep moving. Maria Harrison, sis, I love you for always being an ear when I vent and always encouraging me to move on. Tierra Sims, man from day one you been my hitta, and I love your mean ass forever in a day. Chante Amor (Jessica) it's hard because I miss you most talking to me with the dog barking and Joyce tryna come visit and laughing about the dumbest shit. My cousin, Shay, we being brave together deciding to write because we know we got skills. To my readers thanks for riding for me, so I'mma write for you.

PROLOGUE

Devin "Demon" Coles

Fifteen years old

Bang. Bang. Bang. Was all I heard.

Whoever the fuck it was had to be one determined ass nigga. It had been a week since I had left the apartment. A smell lingered throughout the house, and it could only be from one room because every other room I made sure to clean from top to bottom. I just could not find the strength to enter in there. If I did, it would be like I was wiping away her existence, and as bad as I acted, letting, go of my old girl was something I could not do. I swung the door open to a worried Juniece. You could tell she had been crying in a tight spandex shirt and shorts with a messy bun on top of her head. Even at fifteen, Juniece was thicker than most, but you could never deny her beauty. Part of me always thought she was too good for me. Yet whether its friendship or relationship, she always chose me without a second thought.

"You missed school again... I bought your homework that you missed and some food I experimented with. Tell me if you like it."

Nodding my head, I lifted the top on the bowl to see lasagna with homemade garlic bread. That is Juicy though she always cared about others before herself. She could cook you anything and it would taste like an everyday meal "it smells like an app in here. Ass, piss, and pussy," Juniece yelled at me. I said nothing as I looked her up and down with her shorts cling to her ass, showing her pussy print, and it made me jealous.

"It's their room. I couldn't face going in there to clean up."

"Go eat I'll take care of it."

"I can clean it up. I got to face it some time."

"Devin, go eat now. I am not anybody. My mom is coming over to talk with you," Juniece said before she grabs all the cleaning products I had.

It took a whole hour before she came and asked if I could help her with my parent's bed that we were throwing out. By the time we were finished. Ms. Julissa was already knocking on the door. She had bags in her hand and before she could ask for help, I was already taking them out here hand.

"Thank you, baby. After you put up the groceries, I want you to come sit down so we can talk."

"Yes ma'am," I replied, putting up all the meats and veggies and refrigerator foods.

"You're a man now that's what you think, huh?"

"Not at all! I'm learning to stand on my own."

"Good answer. I was on my own at an incredibly young age. it was hard until I had met my husband. People see a person being lost as a weakness. That will not happen on my watch. My daughter loves you and the friendship the both of you have created. Your mom also came to me and asked that if anything happened to her. look after you. The apartment is in my name and yours. So, on school days. you stay with us and weekends, you can spend here long as you abide by the rules I set until you come of age."

"Ms. Julissa, I appreciate the offer but."

"But what? Here's my proposition. You go to school, long as you maintain good grades, I will allow freedom within reason. I will pay the bills and utilities and groceries and any other things you require. Whatever odds jobs you do to make money is yours. Learn to save and to be independent. We decorated the basement for you with a brand-new wardrobe.

"You did not have to do that."

"I know I didn't, but I did. See, all your life you have been by yourself, and that time is over whether you like it or not, we're family and we're here to stay. So have ya ass in through those doors during curfew or else."

"Yes ma'am."

After Ms. Julissa left. Juicy and I chilled and reminisced until it was time to go home. It was weird but their place always felt more like a home than mine. The first night we ordered pizza and Juicy passed out after her shower while I ended up watching *Four Brothers* with Ms. Julissa.

"I know I have yet to say, it but I'm sorry about your parents."

"It's cool. Everyone dies, right."

"Everyone dies that's true, but it still hurts, nonetheless. You can be angry or mad at a person who died and still miss them." She spoke, pulling me into a big warm hug. It was a mom's hug and it reminded me that I did not have one because she died, and I missed her. Every day I put up a front but, in all reality, it was breaking my heart.

"I hate my old man for taking my ole girl away from me and leaving me without. I hate that I must learn what a real man is from everyone but him. I hate that my mother was so weak. Why couldn't she just take me and leave? Maybe the everything wouldn't hurt so bad." I spoke through my tears while Ms. Julissa rubbed my back.

"Only she knows that but D, you have to understand that no matter what she loved you."

"I know that."

"Then make her proud and do all the things she couldn't. Now that she free she everywhere you are so making every experience count."

"I will. I think I'm going to go to bed."

"Okay. Goodnight, D."

"Goodnight." I replied before laying in the bed and thinking of my mother. I had so much regret. I should have been stronger; she should've left yet those were my opinions. I could not imagine walking her shoes. Still, I missed that woman every moment of the day.

Juniece

It was last period, and I had so much to do. Bitches talked shit about how fat I was, niggas were stone cold faking like they didn't enjoy the sight, and teachers passing out way too much homework on a damn Friday. Thank God this was my last year in this high school. Just as I was about to raise my hand to be excused the bell rung, just as quick I grabbed my bag and went to my locker to grab the books. I needed to study with over the weekend. I had four projects and I wanted to get a head start on it. The one thing that my mom didn't play with was my schooling because she always said dummy's skip school and look like a fool but ones that learn could run the world. It was corny but where was the lie though? Too many girls in my school were already pregnant by these lame ass niggas, and I refused to be another one.

"Juicy when you are going to let a nigga take you out on a date?" Michael a kid from class asked. He was the cockiest nigga I knew and honestly, I didn't know why. He hated Demon and always found ways to use me to make him jealous. It never worked but nonetheless it was irritating.

"You know I got a boyfriend, so that's a no go," I replied and continued to keep walking. The look on his face told it all, he was embarrassed, but I couldn't have cared less. Michael was an attention seeker and a straight dumbass and most importantly, not worth my time. I only started dating a few months ago and even Duke was working my last nerves.

"How a fat bitch like you thinks she sexy, I'll never understand. Shit, I just wanted some head anyway and to see how wide that pussy is." Michael's words angrily spewed from his mouth before he even thought about it.

Just as he was about to offer up a bullshit apology, I said forget it. It wasn't even like Michaels' words affected me because unlike others. I knew my worth. I also knew there was a bet going around school for three hundred dollars to the boy that I let hit. Of course, my bestie. Demon, found out and got suspended for knocking the teeth out the last two niggas who attempted to spit game my way. Instead of replying to Michael's bitter ass, I walked to my car that Demon bought last year for my seventeenth birthday. It wasn't much. but I appreciated it, nonetheless. Opening the door to my silver 2017 Toyota Camry, I grabbed my phone off the seat to make a call anytime he wasn't there. After three rings, he picked up.

"Baby girl, where you at?" Devin's deep baritone voice blasted through the phone, sending chills up my spine whenever I heard his voice. Demon had a voice that didn't match his looks. He was always a thinker but fuck with him. He could be the coldest nigga especially if it was someone close to his heart.

"Leaving school, on my way home. You know my momma leaving today for her business trip. so, I can stay over this weekend."

Devin lived in the apartments on Suitland Road, in a two bedroom. It was decked out from the front to the back the living room was crème and gold with black accents to match. Just like the living room, the dining room had the same type of feel just with burnt orange and brown. I loved his apartment so much because it always felt like I was living in a Picasso painting with all the bright colors. The rooms were even better because one was mine. His had a forest green and black color scheme with a king size bed, whereas mine was red and black with a queen size.

Everyone thought we were sleeping together but that was further from the truth. Even his girlfriend looked at me sideways because anytime they were at the mall, Devin would cop me something too. Anything I wanted I got. Since the day he walked into my life he always found a way to make me smile.

We had just moved to Maryland when my mom had got word that my dad got killed on active duty. The army came with a folded flag and a medal telling my mother about his bravery but that wasn't what I wanted to hear. I stood at the door waiting for him to come and scream sike and hold me and tell me all the things he did anytime he came home. Instead, I sat on the porch wanting to cry. Just as looked up a boy about the same age as I walked up to the house directly across the street from our new home. The-nappy--headed boy placed a bag on the porch and let it on fire, then rang the doorbell and ran. The old lady started stumping on it to put the fire out, only to she realizes it was shit inside. The boy stood from the bushes, holding his stomach laughing.

"Demon you a bad little bastard!" the lady screamed as he flipped her the finger, screaming suck his dick all while crossing the street.

"Hey that was mean," I expressed. Back then, I wasn't nothing but a shy girl too scared to stand up on her own yet being around him gave me the courage to do anything including standing up to him.

"Who asked you, and why are you sitting there all sad and shit with your lip all poked out."

"My daddy died. People always leaving me."

"Me too. The name's Devin but as the parents around here call me, Demon."

"I'm Juniece but everyone calls me Juni for short."

"Naw, that ain't gonna work for me. I'm special, so I want to give you my own name. Stand up and turn around and let me look at you,", he demanded. He stares made me so uncomfortable that for a second, I trembled.

"You always been chubby?"

"Yea, I guess?" I asked with just a hint of insecurity.

"Don't do that."

"Do what?" I asked.

"If I offended you, speak up, even though I didn't mean to. I think you're pretty, but that's too common, I'mma call you Juicy."

"I guess."

"Come on let me show you around." Devin suggested, and I followed. From that day, we'd been each other's keepers.

"Can you roll thru and cook a nigga a warm meal?" Devin asked, making me giggle inside, bringing me out my thoughts.

Demon was greedy as they came. Even though I knew I needed to study because finals were coming up, there was no way I would tell him no.

"Yea, be there after Mom leave and make sure the stuff is on the counter, thawed out," I replied before hanging up the phone, pulling out the parking space. I didn't live far from the school, so I got there in no time. Soon as I entered my house, I saw my mom pulling her luggage down the stairs.

"Hey," Juni My mom said, calling me by my childhood nickname.

"Hey, Momma."

"I thought I wasn't going to see you, but I left money on the counter. Are you staying home or going to the apartment?" my mom asked.

She, like everybody else, thought me and Devin had something going on especially after he purchased me a car and put my name on the lease. But I was the only family Devin had next to his cousin, Kano. Now I would be lying if I said I wasn't attracted to him. Demon is one of them too fine to be mine type of guys. I never forget how she caught us in the bed and overreacted by taking me to the doctors only to find out I was still a virgin. Which I still am embarrassed to this day. I wasn't waiting on Mr. Right nor was I hoping for the perfect moment. I just couldn't vibe with nobody but Devin and unfortunately, I was too scared to go there.

"Yea, I came to shower then I'm heading there before it gets dark."

"Okay. Be safe, Jun. See you in a week. Tell Devin to call me back too. I Love you." My mom replied, kissing my forehead, and leaving out.

Stripping out of my clothes, I turned the shower on hot just the way I liked it. After checking to make sure it was just right, I hopped in and cleaned my body with my coconut mango body wash. After scrubbing every inch of my body, I toweled dried my body, applying my lotion all over. Looking through my closet, I opted for a peach romper with my brown gladiator sandals. I pulled my hair in a messy bun, adding some strawberry lip gloss to make my lips pop. After looking in, the mirror and being satisfied with my look, I grabbed my keys, the money my mom gave me, and left out. That's another thing I didn't have to stress about when it came to money 'cause Demon always put fifteen hundred in my account every two weeks even though I barely touched it.

Tonight, Duke and I were going to a late movie. Only thing is I really wasn't feeling in the mood to argue with him again. It was always the same shit different day. Why can't I stay the night? Why do you always run when he calls? Are you fucking that nigga? I hated explaining myself to muthafucka's who didn't really matter. Duke and I been together three months and already felt he loved me and thought we should take it to the next level. Dead. I swear nigga always tried to run game like bitches wasn't hip to their shit. I put on my turn signal to enter in the complex. Soon as cut off the car my best friend Drita yelled at her mom probably for taking the rent money again to get high.

"Dee, calm down, people don't need to be in your business," I said, trying to calm Drita down.

"No Juni, I'm tired of this shit. When we get put out for not paying the rent where we gonna go? This bitch doesn't think about it between paying off her debts to the local drug dealers and necessities, I'm barely surviving. I always got her but damn who got me?" Drita whined in my arms.

"I got you, Dee, come in the house with me. I'll give you the money to pay the rent." I went into the building and open my apartment, smelling the sweet vanilla air freshener fill the room. I went straight to my room and unlocked my door. I opened the wall safe, peeling off six hundred dollars and handed it to Dee.

"Thanks, Juniece, I promise I'm going to pay you back."

"Don't worry about it."

Drita was one of many living in a nice place thanks to section 8 hooking people up like her momma. She always did the best she could do, but life always had a way of breaking her down. I love my girl, and I would never see her on the streets. If I, had it then she had it.

"I gotta get to work. Wanna chill when I get off?"

"Yea. That's fine." When I walked Drita out, Demon and Jessa calm walking down the hall. More like Jezebel if you asked me.

"Juniece, don't you look cute for a big girl. I was just telling friend the other day if you lose 250 pounds, you would be so cute." Bruh, I hate skinny bitches, but Jessa took the cake always throwing shade because the love Demon had for me.

"Nah, baby girl knows her ass is sexy as fuck," Demon spoke, looking in my eyes.

He always reassured me whenever I had doubts that I was the most beautiful and best girl to him. To me, his opinion was the only one that mattered.

"I'm right here."

"And you worried about the wrong shit. Get your stuff so I can take you home."

"Why can't I stay when she stays? What the fuck, are you fucking her or something?"

"First of all, you know damn well when baby girl over here all my time goes to her. Stop trying me, Jessa or you're going to end up being replaced because that girl right there is my heart."

Nothing else needed to be said. Jessa always tried to get a reaction out of me, but in all actuality, Demon wasn't my man. He was my friend. Yea, I'd go to the ends of the earth to protect him and vice versa, but in no way, shape or form would I get in way of his happiness no matter how I felt about her. I went in the kitchen washed my hands and went to work on dinner.

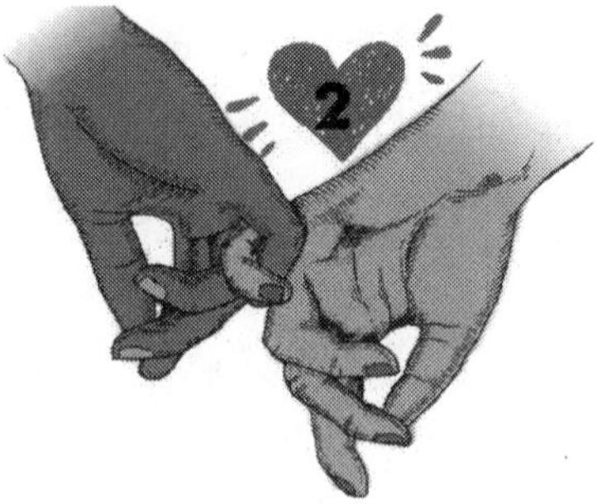

Demon

Here I was stuck in traffic listening to Jessa nag about Juniece for the thousand time. Nobody believed that she and I were just friends and truthfully, I was tired of explaining that shit. Since the day I meet Juicy, I could tell she was special. She made a size twenty look damn good. I confided in her cause she would legit have the answers. Baby girl knew her place in my life and that's why it bothered a lot of people. A lot of people assume that they knew what I was into, but they didn't at all. People swore I sold drugs and was a kingpin because I would chill with my cousin, Kano, and shit. I was sixteen when my cousin offered me a job with this lady named J.B. She was so impressed at how fast I learned that she offered me a job as her partner once I finished college. I made great grades that I could get into any school on the planet. For now, though I was fine being an arms dealer in training. I had street smarts and book smarts so with all that, I knew I also know there was more to learn.

I didn't have nobody in this world who gave me as much as Juniece. I was on my own since I been fourteen and survival is some fucked up shit when you're a kid. My dad was chasing his next high that he never came back to make sure a nigga was good. The next day, I found out that my dad beat my mother to death then overdosed right next to her. I had no feelings about the shit because I felt like life got the best of them. The rent was only twenty-five dollars, both parents were still getting food stamps, and the government still sent out utility checks. I guess they was still too lazy to close the case after Ms. Julissa took them their death certificates. They had me when they were kids themselves. Their parents were shit; mines were shit, but I was changing that cycle. There I was in a low-income apartment with no food and an adult's responsibilities. Nobody cared for kids like me but Ms. Julissa and Juniece. From the time we met, she rode for ya boy when nobody else would. When her mom went shopping for her house, she would take food and the necessities to stock up my house. She got cookbooks from the library to make me special meals whenever I did good in school. She made me study, never giving up faith that I could be something better than I was.

I remember my first Christmas without my parents. It must off really hit home because I cried almost the whole day. Juicy spent that morning with her mother and told her she was spending the night at her friend's house but was really with me. We spent the three hours at the grocery store on Christmas Eve pushing groceries home just so she could cook for Christmas. It was perfect baked mac and cheese, stuffed chicken, honey glazed ham, homemade greens, yams with the brown sugar and marshmallows, potato salad, with cornbread that looked like pound cake and banana pudding. It was nothing more she could give me, right? Wrong. She used all the gift cards she had to buy me shoes and clothes and not once threw none of that shit in my face. She just wanted to give me the world without anything in return. When I got straight still, she didn't ask for shit, so I took the place as her man even before I knew what that meant.

"Devin, do you hear me?"

"Look why does she bother you so much?"

"Because you love her that's why."

"Cause she's my best friend."

"Nah nigga not like that. The way you look at her like she is the only person in this world can keep you calm. When you mention her name, you smile so hard like nothing else matters but her. We been together two years, and not once have you cared enough the way you do her. So, if I'm jealous it's because you created it," Jessa vented.

It fucked me up inside because I cared for Jessa but instead of concentrating on us, she'd rather take someone else's place. I got mad love for Jessa, and I wasn't sure if I was willing to let go just yet.

"What do you want me to do, man?"

"If there's nothing going on, then I want to stay a week with you; the way we are when she at home with her mom. I want to solidify my part in your life."

"Fine, man, go ahead and get your shit, and I'll be down here waiting."

"Yessssss!" Jesscenda squealed running into her apartment building not before laying a soft ass kiss on my lips. I got in my truck and called Juicy, who picked up on the first ring.

"What you did?" she said as soon as she picked up.

Juicy had this baby voice that was sexy as shit on her. Even though I refuse to take it there, a blind man could see baby girl was beyond real. She was who I saw growing old with. Arguing with, taking adventures with. With her I saw past, present, and future. That girl was going to be my wife.

"Girl, nothing. Check this out tho, Jessa staying the week with us."

"Ok, Devin, dinners done. I'll set a place for her before I leave out," she replied with a hint of disappointment behind it.

"You not staying in?" I asked, hoping she would catch on and change her mind.

"No, I'mma chill with Duke tonight and see you at eleven for our ritual. I'll let anything slide but that."

"I got you, bae. I'll see you later." I replied before hanging up.

After five minutes, Jessa came out dressed like she was queen of the streets or some shit. She had on black jeans with a gold and black top with a crown and some heels. Don't get me wrong, the shits were straight sexy but over the top. I helped her with her bag and hopped in as she waited me to open her door. Instead. I ignored her ass until she finally gave in and got her ass in the car.

"Can we go to Outback? I want their wings."

"Nah, Juicy cooked, and I don't feel like eating out tonight anyway."

"It's amazing. If Juicy fat ass said let's go out, you all for it, but if I ask… you're tired." Jessa nagged, fucking up my mood.

"I might've didn't want to hang up what we had just yet, but insulting baby girl was a big ass No, no in my book. I grabbed Jesscenda by her neck, adding pressure. Not enough to kill her but still hard enough to get my point across.

"Them fat jokes better leave ya small ass brain of yours. I don't cheat on you, fuck other bitches, I give you money and you're still threatened by a girl who can't care less about you. Fix that shits quick or jump out my ride.... Your choice," I expressed as she tried to catch her breath.

Ten minutes in, nothing was said nor did her dumbass get out, so I started my truck up and sped down the street listening to Jay Z 's new album. I really fucked with that song 'The story of O.J' 'cause at the end of the day, we still niggas just in different colors. We didn't get in the house four anther forty-five minutes due to traffic. Niggas couldn't drive for shit. Sometimes, I wondered how they got their license. Soon as we got in, I ran to the kitchen to see if my food wrapped up. Looked everywhere. I entered the dining room to a candlelight dinner.

"This is so beautiful. Devin." Jessa cooed.

"I don't know the fuck why; I didn't do this shit," I replied, picking up a paper with Juniece's handwriting on it."

Devin,

I went on a date with Duke, dinner is in the oven, it's all your favorites. Cajun shrimp and

chicken alfredo with Caesar salad and garlic bread.

Also, Jessa, I know you like wine there's a chilled bottle of Sweet Red in the fridge. See you later.

-Juicy

"That was sweet of her." Jessa said with a hint of sarcasm.

She was starting to really blow me that the whole time we ate in silence. There wasn't shit to say as far as I was concerned. I cleaned up the kitchen and went to take a nice, hot shower. The water was hot you would have thought I was in a sauna. When I got out, the clock read ten. Going over to my dresser. I grabbed me a pair of boxers and my playboy pajama pants. I went over to my bed to grab my phone to text baby girl. Jesscenda was knocked out sleep in my bed without washing her ass. If there was one thing, I hated it was outside smells on my sheets. Deciding to just let her sleep. I went on about my merry way. Not three minutes later, I got a call from baby girl saying she was in her room about to take a shower and be out after that. I grabbed two coolers and the gummy bears and chips and set everything on the floor and started the game. When I looked up there, she was with her ponytail in a messy bun with a small ass tank top and shorts accompanied by that damn tinker bell blanket she loved so much. She motioned for me to open my legs so she can sit between them. She smelled so good that I swore she caught me sniffing her.

"Okay, what game are we learning tonight?" She laid her head on my chest. Every time Juniece learned a game, a new system would come out, and I would get the shit. Since the PS4 came out, we been playing that shit like crazy.

"GTA," I replied just like any girl she found a store and started buying shit. I opened our drinks and watched until she needed me. This space is where with Juicy is where I wanted to be. "Bruh, use the controls to drive, you are running over people and shit."

"Look, don't make me hit you."

"Whatever, so how was your date tonight?" I asked.

"Same ole thing. It's like he doesn't trust me around you. Tonight, tho we argued, and I swear I was tired of defending us to everybody including him so when he asked me was it a future him or the friend zone with you …."

"Who did you choose? I know what we got, so if he makes you happy that's all I care about."

"You, I chose you 'til the casket drops." She turned around, placing the sweetest kiss on my lips. It wasn't nothing like we shared before; this wasn't no simple peck that we always did. This kiss had meaning behind it.

She slid her tongue in my mouth as I awaited and accepted it, tasting the sweetness from the candy she had at prior. We kissed a whole five minutes before we remembered that what we were doing was wrong. For me Juicy was the end game, and I was not ready to love her the way she needed me to. Although it hurt, I would protect this girl from anyone including me.

"Juicy…"

"We can't..." she mumbled before getting up to go to her room without so much as a goodnight.

That shit that went down fucked me up in more ways than one. I wanted to go there but that meant I could possibly fuck up what we had, knowing that I could never take it there. I got to my bedroom, sliding right under Jessa thinking about Juicy.

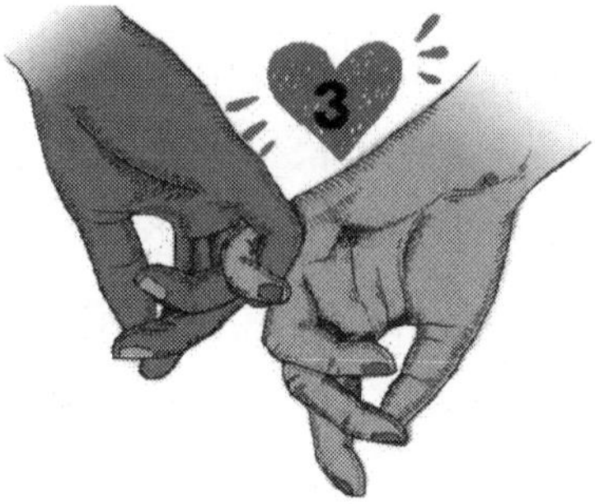

Drita

"Drita, you have people at table three," the girl, Crystal, announced while I was putting on my apron.

Lately everything had me feeling like I was drowning. This job was a dead end, and my mother even though I hate to say it would be dead soon. She kept taking drug on credit from the local dealers, knowing I would pay the shit but, how sway? It's a damn shame I had to depend on Juniece to help just to get by. My name is Drita Mathews. I graduated from high school last year and truthfully, college was the furthest from my mind and barely got out of there. I'd been at Red Lobster for two years and everyday it was always a muthafucka trying me. I walked over to the table and there was a group of fine ass niggas that occupied it. I was sure they were some dogs and no way I tryna to go smack at either of them, but it was nice to admire the fine specimen that sat before me.

"Welcome to Red Lobster, my name is Drita, and all be serving you today. Can I start you off with any drinks today?"

"Let us all get four Malibu Hurricanes, sweetheart," the guy replied with his head down.

When he lifted his head and smiled them damn pearly whites in my face, it was over. I thought for sure you could see the drool from the corners of my mouth."

"And are you ready to order, yet or do you need some more time?"

"We ready," they all replied. One by one, they ran down their order 'til it got to daddy.

I stood there, waiting with my handy dandy notebook and pen like I was about to take the most important dictation of my life. "I'll take the crab legs and trio shrimp, and can I get some mayonnaise, ketchup, and mustard please," he said. I swear I was all goofy=eyed. Getting my composure, I left to put the orders in.

"Bitch. I see you like that table, huh," Crystal commented with her nosey, hoe ass. I trusted none of these bitches, but out of all of them Crystal was the most tolerable.

"They cute or whatever," I replied, grabbing their plates while she assisted with the drinks.

I placed everything down on the table, then I walked away, allowing them to eat in peace. I checked on my other tables but for some reason I felt like someone was watching me. I turned around and there he was, watching me as our eyes connected. Grabbing the bill, I placed in next to him. Just I was about to walk away. he grabbed my arm. sending chills up my spine. He pulled out a wad on money placing ten crisps one hundred-dollar bills down then handed that and the bill to me. Lord knows I needed the money and even if I tried to give Juni the money back. she wouldn't take it. So, I guess I could pay to some bills and groceries in the house, nonetheless I was appreciative. She saw the real me and had my back since the day we met; she has been there for all my shit and vice versa. Like Meredith and Christina from *Grey's Anatomy*, she was my person.

"Miss!" a lady called from my other table.

The ghetto hoes were hating because none of the guys at the table seemed to give them the time of day. When I went back to the table, they were gone, but the receipt said call him and had his number. I blushed because even though I needed the money, I really needed to open a bank account before I choked my mother to death. Nothing else eventful happened. Bout time I finished my shift, all I wanted to do was curl up in my bed and sleep Thank God, I was off tomorrow. Deciding to cut my phone on. I watched the text messages come through.

Juni Bae: Tonight, was the night I broke up

With Duke. Sis calls me.

Juni Bae: OMG!!!!!! I kissed him and it was, Perfect boo. Now it's awkward.

Juni Bae: I'm freaking out Dee, I love him.

I read in awe, it wasn't no secret how Demon and Juniece felt about each other but never in a million years would I think Juni would act on it. I admired the connection they had together.

Me: Just got off work, I'll be home in 15 minutes.

Open the door.

I hopped in my Uber and was home in no time. I didn't even bother going in the house to check on my mom. Nine times out of ten, she was entertaining the local addicts. I know I may seem harsh, but even with all the love I had for my mom, I was tired. My dad never cared for me; that fool ran off and had a new family while we struggled. Before he left my mom was fine, now she was becoming more and more a pain in my ass. I let myself in the apartment and went straight to Juni's room where she was on the bed studying with tears falling.

"Aww, boo don't cry." I comforted her, patting her on her back.

"How could something be so perfect. Dee, and be so wrong?" she asked, whimpering.

"Juniece, for as long as I can remember y'all been best friends, that man has confided in you, defended you, and loved you above anybody else, and tonight, you acted on your feelings without thinking about the damage it could do to the relationship that you two have."

"I know, Dee, I just can't hide my feelings no more. He does everything a man does for a woman he's love. What's wrong with me? Is it my weight?"

"Even you don't believe that. He's not that guy, boo, and you're not that girl. He cares about your feelings that I think he rather proceed with caution. You have never doubted your weight before don't start now," I spoke.

I meant every word. Juniece was beautiful inside and out. She didn't need no confirmation from no one. I set and held her 'til she fell asleep. I got up a went to the drawer she had for me and went to the bathroom to shower. My Cherry Blossom body wash from Bath and Body Works was everything, it was my favorite scent. I scrubbed my body from that seafood smell from work. Hopping out the shower, I placed my hair in a messy bun 'til I could get to the shop and brushing my teeth. When I opened the door, Jessa was there smiling in my face.

"Can I help you?" I asked.

"No," she replied. all devious and shit.

“Then move,” I demanded as Jessa stepped to the side.

“Oh, for the record tell your little friend he will never choose her fat ass.”

“Why are you worried. Jesscenda? I know… it because you know just like I know that his heart belongs to her. He might not act on those feelings, but you know your days are numbered.”

“He won’t leave his family for her. I’m pregnant.”

“Funny you mention that ‘cause word around town is you been being extra friendly with Mac on the eastside. He’s been telling anyone who’d listen that his girl about to have a baby.”

“With you knowing all this why don’t you tell Devin or Juniece? It’s kind of fake don’t you think?”

“No, see females like you get what’s coming to them without anyone having to intervene. A snake in the grass only gets you so far before you realize you can’t expect to have happiness while making others miserable. All I can do is warn him but knowing my bro he has a plan already."

"Well, aren't you the little fortune cookie. I've always landed on my feet just like me and Devin will always be back together.... Goodnight," she said, pushing me out her way.

After flipping through the channels, all I could think about was the guy from my job. Something told me to put it in my phone, but I had yet to call or text. Part of me was scared that he'd treat me as another female to fuck and another part of me wanted to explore the possibilities. Throwing caution to the wind, I decided to send him a text.

Me: Wyd?

Ole Sexy Ass: I see your lil ass finally decided.to use that number. What took, you so long?

Me: Do you even know who this is?

Ole Sexy Ass: There isn't but a few people got my personal number, Drita. What ya fine ass doing anyway?"

Me: Flipping channels bored.

Ole Sexy Ass: It's late take your ass to sleep. Meet me for breakfast in the morning if you ain't scared.

I didn't even reply because I was cheesing so damn hard and hesitant all at the same time. For the reminder of the night, I caught up on Game of Thrones and Power since I didn't have cable, so I binge watched TV' til I fell asleep or so I thought.

Mookie drug addict: ya momma over here trying to pop your room door. Get over here before she sells your shit again like last time.

Me: coming now.

Throwing my sweats on. I walked to my apartment. Soon as I got in the apartment, I knew I was going to be some shit. Standing butt ass naked in the middle of the floor high as hell singing the P-Valley song using a broom to ass the poll. I couldn't do shit but shake my head. To be clear, my mother had a body on her and even after all the drugs, she was still holding up that she could pull a benefactor quick, but nope this bitch was busting it wide open for some niggas with empty pockets. The room smelled like stale ass and desperation. Walking past her. I saw my room wide open with the jar that I kept my money in, empty. It wasn't all my money just what I had that was easy for her to find. As much as I wanted to fight her, it wasn't worth it. Most of my clothes was at Juniece' house. I packed the rest of my shit prepared to leave.

"DD, where you are going, girl. Look I'm sorry I took ya money. I pay you back."

"With what? I work a dead-end job to pay your bills and debts, and I'm grateful for it, but you need to do better. You steal what little I have for your habit. Ma. what have I done to you to do me this way?" I asked with tears streaming. In all my years I always felt like I had to buy little moments of her love.

"You were born," this bitch had a nerve to say. Bending down, I hugged my naked mother and placed a blanket around her.

"You're so lost, Momma, that I can't be the one to save you anymore. I love you but staying here is killing me. Take care of yourself," I replied before kissing her forehead and walking away while she screamed bullshit to my back. For the first time since I was kid, I felt a weight lifted up of my shoulders.

"Don't be kissing on me. I don't need you, you ungrateful lil' bitch. I gave you life and raised you. The least your ass could do is pay some bills around here and clear my debts. I am your momma after all!" she yelled as a giggle escaped my lips.

"Mom? Ma'am, you use that term too loosely. The only reason you are not being pimped out and beaten is because of me. Since I been eight, I have been cooking and taking care of your ass. Until Demon and Juni, I had to steal and eat to survive. I remember one day you sold all your food stamps; my stomach growled so loud, I missed breakfast, couldn't pay for lunch. I ate food out the dumpster. I was a child, and you were getting high in the process. I'm going to live for me and find out what life has to offer because if I stay, I'll kill you or you'll break me. I'll pay the rent for three more months but after that. I can't help you."

"Drita don't goooooo please…. I….. I…. can't get high without your money." this bitch really had the nerve to say. Not even replying. I went to Juni's house. Hopefully, they would let me stay until I figured things out.

"Take care of yourself, I got her, baby girl." Mookie announced. I gave him a hug. Since I was a baby. Mookie always took care of me. he talked to me about the birds and the bees. He bought me my first pair of pads. He was the closest thing I had to a dad. I appreciated him because he was there when my momma was too high to notice anything.

Juniece

The morning came with the sunlight shinning on my face and truthfully, I did not want to move out of bed. Drita was still sleep from being up all damn night like she was anytime she was over here. I could smell breakfast being cooked. and my stomach grumbled. Pulling myself out of bed, I washed my face and brushed my teeth then left to see what was in stored. Soon as I made it to the kitchen, all the color left my face watching Jezebel and Devin all damn kissy face. Pretending to ignore them. I went in the fridge, pouring me a glass of nice, cold, orange juice.

"Morning, baby girl. I made breakfast; do you want some?" Devin asked. I knew what it was about. He felt guilty about playing me to the left and wanted me to not be mad at him, which I wasn't, I was madder at myself for allowing last night to happen the way it did. Getting up. I fixed me and Drita a healthy plate of bacon, eggs, and hash browns with toast. The whole time I was eating in silence Devin tried talking to me but there wasn't shit to say. I was to embarred and scared he would tell me I wasn't his type or there would never be an us.

"We are hitting up Lux Lounge tonight. Are you coming?" Let us not forget that I been getting into clubs since I was sixteen years old and focus on the fact this nigga just asked me lowkey to be a third wheel.

“Maybe some other time, Drita and I are going to the mall and then I’m going home to wash clothes and study.

“You are coming back tomorrow, right?” he asked.

“Nah, I’mma just chill at home ‘til my mother gets back.”

“Uh hmm, Jessa, let me holla at Juicy really quick. Matter fact, go get ready. I’mma take you to the mall.”

“Okay, Daddy,” Jessa responded, placing a kiss on his lips, switching her hips from side to side.

“Baby girl, what’s your problem?”

“Nothing, I just got a lot of studying to do and being here can be a distraction.” I replied, fidgeting.

He walked over to me and cuffed my chin, staring his deep brown eye into mine. "Do you think I'm stupid? You been my A1 since Day 1, so I know when something's wrong. Speak that shit or get over that fucking attitude."

"I want what you have with her, I want what I felt last night with you," I pleaded as Devin rubbed his hands down his face.

"Why are you willing to accept pieces of me? I can't give myself to you when a part of me still wants to be with her. Huh? Why is the bare minimum okay with you when there's someone better than me out there?"

"Because in your heart of hearts, you love me more. And in my heart, I know that I can love you better than she can. Trust me when I say this jealousy aside, are you happy with her? No because there's not another bitch on this earth that can be your everything other than me. Devin, if I'm being real, the day; I met you was the moment I fell for you. I'm not delusional either; what we got is rare and you're getting in the way of something great. I know why I never gave Duke a real chance because he could never be you. When we kiss, to how we talk to one another, to how we ride for each other speaks volumes." I said breathing heavy, moving closer to him.

"Juicy, man. that don't mean shit." Demon whispered. pulling me into his chest. I inhaled his scent. It was so intoxicating that I placed a soft kiss on his exposed area.

"It does, Devin. Since we were kids, I've watched you with female after female and supported you good, bad, indifferent, and with each one none of them none made you happy. If they did, I'd be your best man cheering you on, yet I know the truth. You love me." I touched his face, placing a kiss on his lips.

"Baby girl don't do this." he asked, gripping my waist tighter and kissing me deep. In his eyes. though I saw the turmoil and to the hand that I was dealt. I also wasn't willing to fold.

"Do what? All this time. you don't know me by now. I need space for now. When I'm ready. I'll be back," I replied and went to my room.

Of course, Drita ass wasn't sleep. she waited as I handed her a plate while I went to shower. 'Bout time I got out. the plate was empty, and Drita was walking to hop in. It was hot outside. Instead of wearing jeans, I opted for my ripped distressed shorts and my white halter shirt with my classic princess Reebok. Say whatever you wanted about those shoes. but they reminded me of my childhood when things were simple between Demon and me.

"You like?" Drita asked. standing in the doorway with a white romper with some muti color Gucci slides and purse I bought her last year for her birthday which was coming up soon. She and Kano had the same birthday. so, Demon decided we should throw their party together.

"Bishhh yass you look sexy as fuck."

"Tell me anything," she taunted.

"Come on, we got to finish buying the rest of our stuff for our trip Monday." I replied. Since Demon and I were seniors and caught up on all our assignments. we were allowed to attend senior ditch week.

We hit every store imaginable; it didn't even matter that I spent almost twenty thousand in less than two hours. The smile on Drita's face made me happy to spoil my girl. It was all about her and Kano, she of course thought we was we was going to just dinner, but it was her nineteenth birthday, and I wanted to turn up.

"So, who else is coming?"

"Duke, Jezebel, Chance, Lyric, Nexus, and Luka."

"You seriously bringing that dirty q-tip."

"Yea. I don't want to be around D and his hoe all by myself. and I truly need to decide if this is the end of us or can we repair what we have." I hated that Duke always tried to make me choose. but he wasn't all bad he made me smile and laugh when he didn't let his jealousy overpower our relationship. I wasn't stupid; if he wasn't fucking me, he was fucking somebody. I just never cared to ask. It was hard to trust any man outside my circle of friends.

"I understand that and know I got your back. sis." Drita said, hugging me.

"Thanks."

"Wait who the hell decided to invite the Wu Tang crew?"

"Bruhh, Chance and Lyric aren't that bad." I giggled.

"I'm not talking about Chance. I'm talking about the cousins. Lyric and Nexus crazy ass. Every time they link up. it's pandemonium. Last time a female smiled at that boy. Them girls whooped that girl ass so bad and all she was doing was trying to sell that damn perfume at Macy's."

"That girl had a smart mouth; she shouldn't have said what she said. That's what was started the whole thing in motion. Plus, it didn't help that she use to fuck Chance hoe ass either," I replied.

"Yea you're right, poor tink, tink never had a chance." Drita giggled.

"Have you talk to your mom yet?"

"No, but I saw Miss Denise yesterday, and she told me the apartment across the hall opened up on a special. I put the application in right there and got approved. I ran so fast to get my debit card in your safe to pay the first month's rent and security deposit." Drita said, beaming proudly. She worked her ass off and saved all her money. instead buying a car. any money she got and put away. She knew that living with her momma would one day lead her down this road. That's why anything she needed me for, I was there. Shit, that went for my girls Lyric and Nexus too.

"Congratulations, boo. When do you move in?"

"Friday. I already went to a furniture store and got majority of the things I need. I'mma ask Demon, Chance, and Luka to come and assemble everything."

"Why didn't you tell me? I would have helped you so you can save."

"That's just it though, I can't keep expecting you to help me. I got to sink or swim on my own. I want to walk beside you and not be a charity case. I'm older than you, I am the big sister," she whined.

What Drita failed to realize we was family and blood couldn't make us any closer. There were plenty of times she slapped a hoe for disrespecting me or yelled at a nigga who called me anything but my name. She felt like she owed me. but everything I'd done was because her friendship, love, and loyalty was worth way more.

"D, we don't see you like that, but I understand. Are you ready for the trip?"

“Am I? Girl, my boss really had the nerve to ask me to come in for three days of my vacation. I told him I’ll pass because I never called in sick, never left early, and always pulled doubles. I need this.”

“And what did he say?”

“See you in two weeks.”

“I bet he did. They need to make you a manger already.”

“Who are you telling?”

We laughed and chopped it up while shopping. When we were done, I loaded all the bags in the trunk and dropped Drita off at her cousin’s house near her job which wasn’t too far from Devin’s and I’s apartment I was so exhausted that I wouldn’t be able to make it home at all. I put on my lock on my car and went in the apartment that Demon and I shared so as I opened the door there, he was sitting on the couch with a drink in his hand. I didn't even stay anything. I just proceeded to my room.

"Can we talk?"

"Nah, where your girl at?" I said through clenched teeth I was lowkey still hurt and embarrassed that he rejected my love as he chuckled a little bit. Even with all that was going on, he still gave me butterflies.

"She went out with her cousin because I sent her home."

"Cool," I replied and continued to my room.

"Juicy..." was all he could get out.

"Devin, not right now. I want is to wash my ass and go to bed. Whatever you want doesn't matter. Please continue drinking, Goodnight."

I entered in my room and ran my water in my whirlpool tub then added some Calgon in the water before placing on the jets and placing my hair in a messy bun. Once I was in, I laid back trying to escape all my insecurities and problems, even though it didn't last long as Devin came waltzing in. He didn't say anything. He washed my body with so much care and massaged my shoulders. Tears fell, and I could not tell you why. I loved him, and I hated him. I needed him one minute, and the next I was over him, that's the control he had over me. Releasing the water out the tub, I turned the shower on and washed my body without saying a word. Devin grabbed a towel and held it open for me, waiting.

"Come on, so I can put some oil on your skin." I stood up and snatched the towel from his hands.

"I know you can't pick me up with your boney ass, so you are making walk to the bed with your weak ass." In an instant, my ass was up in the air and the look on his face made it look like he was picking my ass up with ease. When we got to the bed, he threw my ass so fast not ‘cause my ass was heavy but because I knew what buttons to push. Devin hated when I talked about my weight. He loved all of me. but the fact that he wouldn’t choose me made me doubt all that.

“Juniece I’mma say this shit for the last time, baby girl, ain’t nothing wrong with your weight, but if you don’t like it change it. You’re beautiful down to your soul. There’s no competition when it comes to you. Skinny or thick. you are completely perfect to me.” He stated matter-of-factly.

“You make me this way.” I continued to cry.

“I have never lied to you. Baby girl. you just hated the truth. You gonna always have me.”

“Devin, just go away please. Leave me alone.”

He didn't listen nor did he think about it. Instead, he started touching and sucking on my nipples. A low moan escaped my lips. He traced my body. learning each curve 'til he found my Hershey pot. The kisses Devin planted was so soft and gentle that it sent a fire through my body. My center yearned for his touch.

"Sluuuushhhh!" I screamed out as he slurped my pussy, giving me the first real tongue lashing of my life. With each release, I begged him to stop yet I craved more. My body reacted to his touch like magnets.

"How that shit feel? Baby, talk to me."

"Feels so good, daddy, I'm about to cum again."

"Then, let me taste that sweetness," Demon demanded, inserting a finger in my pussy then another while sucking until the cream released on his tongue.

When he finally came up for air, I kissed that man. tasting my juices on his thick lips and tongue. After going to get a wet rag to clean me off. he climbed in my bed facing me, pulling in his embrace.

"Make love to me. baby." I begged. I was so scared that this was a dream and that making love to me was reassurance.

"Juicy. go your ass to sleep now this isn't the time. Accept what I'm able to give right now." Laughing, I placed a kiss on his lips, getting comfortable. That night, I slept in my man's arms and made a promise to myself that he was my past and my future. Never let another bitch decide how you should feel about a nigga. Thank God Drita decided to babysit her little cousin tonight because I craved this and now, I wanted it.

Drita

it's been two weeks since I moved out. my mom's apartment and truthfully, the money I had saved allowed me to get an apartment across the hall from Demon and Juni's apartment. It was a one-bedroom, two-bath. Thanks to me working since sixteen and not having high bills, I was able to save a pretty penny. And buy some cheap but nice and comfortable furniture from JMD. So, I was happy for the most part. I was always working; I didn't go out much. Unless it was with my friends, and I never had to pay for anything. I was the only single one out the group, so the men always paid for everything because they never wanted me to feel bad. Little did they know, I already was, and I wanted to change that. I was just tired; I wanted so much for myself and kept putting my dreams off for my mother.

I never really thought college was for me. Talking to Kano was like a breath of fresh air. He didn't make me feel less than I was worth, and he prayed with me on our late-night talks and encouraged me when I had so many doubts about taking business courses at the Bowie State college. We had yet to go on a date because of my work schedule, so video chatting was the next best thing. Something about the way he spoke to me always made me wet that after our video chats. I would use my rose toy in my king size platform bed. Only thing I had left to do was find a used car for a reasonable price. Tonight, was my day off. so, I decided to cook stuffed salmon, homemade turnip greens. with sesame rice. and I had a nice cup of red wine with it. When I finished, I checked my phone to see I had a missed call from Kano and ended up calling him back.

"Hey, Beautiful, how was your day?"

"Productive, I registered for classes, went to the grocery store, finished unpacking, and even cooked dinner. How's your day going?"

"Not bad. Handling business as always."

"Kano, you never told me what you do for a living."

"Drita. If I talked about what I do, baby, you would be every bit of mine and would ride this dick every night and sleep in my embrace with ya ass pushing in my dick and be a nigga's peace when I wake up holding you. So, understand that is what it means to know about what I do."

"What if I told you I don't mind the sound of that," I responded, breathing a little funny.

"I would say you better make dame sure. Drita, see the moment a nigga saw you; I saw potential. You could be everything a nigga never thought he needed and everything I craved and wanted at the same time."

"Those are words I heard a lot in my life. Somehow, I'm always left disappointed and alone."

"Yea they words that I can back up. My birthday next week and my cousin going on a trip. Why don't you come too?"

"Can't, my bestie has got something planned already for my birthday next week. We can link up when I get back though."

"Cool with me. Look. I gotta run. I'll see you after I get back from my trip," Kano spoke so sure of himself.

My cousin. London, ask me to watch her daughter tonight, so I made sure to smoke before her little ass came because she was bad a hell. Just as she finished, the doorbell rang.

"Hey, Baby D," London happily said, bringing her little cousin in for the warmest hug.

"Hey, Lee -Lee...I missed you. I can't believe it's been so long, and Paris, boo you look so cute."

"I know I do, but why the polish on your feet and nails color chipped and your hair looks like it seen better says. My daddy always said a unkept person is nothing more than a lonely cat woman," Paris' ass spewed, talking about her daddy. That nigga wasn't no looker his damn self. I couldn't see what my cousin even saw in him.

"Paris you better hush before I popped you in ya mouth. What did I tell you to do before we came up here?"

"To mind my manners."

"Right and you're not doing it. I got to go, but let me get any type of bad report, you can consider that birthday cancelled. Baby D, my momma had a dinner party, and she had some pate and crackers left. Its good so. Paris, give me a kiss before I go."

"Okay. Momma." Paris replied. giving her momma a kiss on the cheek before she left. After I locked the door. I went to the counter to taste Auntie Milan's pate."

"If I, was you, I wouldn't eat it.'"

"Why? Your grandma can cook."

"She can cook some things, but that pate ain't nothing but Pop Pop's potted meat 'cause the pate recipe she tried smelled like feet. Then the church bitches don't know what pate is,"

"Your grandma wouldn't do that." I spoke. taking a bite and immediately knew what this child was saying was true." I threw it in the trash because I came too far to eat potted meat again. I cleaned the mess I made in the kitchen. I showered then watched movies with her until she fell asleep. Shortly after that. I fell asleep thinking about Kano words and was I ready to be with him the way he needed. My phone rung and woke me up. Looking over at the clock, it was two in the morning.

"What's wrong," I panicked.

"Nothing's wrong, bae. I just missed you. Open the door," Kano replied.

I slept in the nude. Grabbing my robe, I opened the door jumping in Kano's arms. My legs wrapped around his as I palmed his face, leaning in I kissed that man so deep that a moan escaped our mouth at the same time. He gripped my ass so hard, I let out a whimper.

"That shit hurt."

"Where the fuck your clothes at?"

"Baby. I was on the couch naked. I hate clothes. I missed you," I spoke in a softest tone.

it'd been so long since I gave a man a chance and truthfully. I silently prayed that this man didn't break my heart.

"Why are you on the couch? Who else is here?" he asked curiously.

"My little cousin. I'm watching her for a few days. Did you come here to fuck me or make love to me?"

"Nah not yet, you gotta earn every inch of this big black, fat dick between my legs."

Maybe it was the way he said those nasty ass words while gripping my ass ever so tightly and sucking on my small breast was enough to fill a mouth, but I creamed right on his jeans. Suddenly, all the color drained from my face. I was embarrassed; no man had ever made me cream without penetration or oral.

"I'm sorry," I apologized.

"For what? Matter of fact. let me clean you up so I can head out. You can be too loud though."

"Okay," I replied.

Kano lifted me on his face and licked my kitty without a morsel left. I whimpered and moaned 'til we were both completely satisfied. Bout time we were done. Kano went to bathroom, to freshen up and said his goodbye. When I locked up, I slid down the door. I missed him already. I sat there for a while before I moved. When I did, I freshened up and went to bed after seeing a text saying goodnight. love. *Damn that, man*. I thought. drifting to sleep.

Jesscenda

This baby had me ready to sleep all day. Instead of going out clubbing. I drove to New York with Duke. making deals and chilling like old times. With him. I could be myself and not get judged. With Devin, he constantly told me what I could improve on. I looked good this I know standing 5-foot-4, redbone, curvy shape, with green eyes, a bitch new she was a whole prize. Still, that wasn't enough. In the beginning of Devin and I dating, everything was cool. He would talk about Fatty like they were family, then I found out that they live together, that shit left me flabbergasted. He always put her first, so I did what I did what I do best, found someone to put me first. Who knew that finding that someone would turn into another messy entanglement?

"Baby, wake up and make me something to eat before I leave," Duke demanded, placing kisses on my neck and back, smacking my fat ass and having a moan escape my lips. His touches were always filled with love and admiration for my body. He was a fine specimen too. That smooth chocolate, rich skin. Deep brown eyes and white bright teeth that lit up the room.

"You keep doing that, I don't think I'm going to make it to the kitchen," I replied as he slid his thick dick in my wet. leaking pussy as I gasp for air. Intertwining his fingers on mine. pumping for dear life while I laid on my stomach. moaning because this man was my addiction. I know I was a fucked-up person. but that's not the case. Duke was mine before he even got with her fat body ass. Everyone thought me and Mac was dating. but the truth was he was with my cousin. Sia, and they also had a baby on the way as well.

"Talk to me, bae, tell me I feel better than that lame ass nigga. Tell me how I make you feel," he whispered in my ear.

Duke was jealous of Devin because he was that dude that every girl wanted, but sex wise Devin was better and bigger, but I wasn't crazy enough to tell him that. Still his dick was eight inches, fat with a curve that made my kitty leak from the thought of it, so lil' daddy knew how to scratch my itch.

"Babe, you are so much better than him, daddy, you make me feel so good. I'm about to cum."

"Release that shit then." He based as we came together, and Duke rolled off me. I knew laying down wasn't an option so like always, I licked and sucked the remains off my man's dick and sloppily kissed him. Then, I got up handled my hygiene and made breakfast for us. Since I been staying with Devin, I had not been grocery shopping, so I opted for eggs, turkey bacon, with wheat toast.

"That shit was good, baby. I'll see you later at the cabin. I left you a few extra stacks in your purse just in case you want something." We shared a kiss before he left.

Truthfully, I wanted to break things off with him. and I couldn't do that because then I would be forced to tell the truth which was, I loved him, and I wasn't nowhere ready for that. Duke was in the streets, but he had hella money. Yeah, I was in a relationship with Devin, yet a blind person could see he was in love with Juniece fat, sloppy ass. This baby was becoming more and more of a pain because I couldn't drink. It was Friday and everyone was prepared to go to Deep Creek for Kano and Drita's birthday party. Everyone planned on getting on the road at two, and it was already ten. After handling my hygiene, I picked out a pink and green Nike sweat suit with my lime and pink Nike slides. After straightening up my apartment. I started packing my duffle bag with all the things I needed. When I was done, the clock had read twelve." I decided to Uber over to Devin's house and take a nap 'til it was time to leave. Soon as I arrived, I knew that was impossible because the ghetto crew was already there in the living room and then and there, I knew there was no way I was going anywhere without backup.

I hated Fatty, but the Gross sisters Drita, Lyric, and Nexus got on my last damn nerves, thinking they was better than me. Hell, Drita definitely be frontin' 'cause not only did she not have a man, but sis was also broken as hell. I had my own money but spending men's money made my already tight pussy leaking whenever they swipe them black cards.

Me: You and Mack tryna go to this cabin. with us? I always need backup. We Leave in an hour.

Sia BOO: Yea, I'll pack me and bae stuff. Text an Address.

After sending the address. I put my bags by the door and went in the kitchen to get some orange juice and went straight to Devin's room. I had no desire to go back and forth with dumb ass broads. I heard the snickers but that didn't bother me. See. I been going to school with fat ass and crack babies since fourth grade and even then, I hated them. Fat Ass wasn't like other fat girls; she walked with her head up and had confidence, and I didn't like that people loved being around her. I hated that. Who did she think she was?

Then, there is her best friend who thought she was too good to lose her virginity like the rest of the girls in her class? So naturally. I had my cousin love her and break her sad ass. Their place was beneath me, and they needed to understand that soon as I hit the bed. I was sleep within seconds.

"Why the fuck you worried about what we got going on?" I heard my cousin scream. I jumped up so fast and walked into the living room to see Mack holding her back, and Duke fussing with Lyric's ghetto ass.

"Bae, what the fuck is going on?"

"I know this slut didn't. Who the fuck are you calling bae, Jezebel? You throw that hot pocket to anyone with a little coin, huh?"

"Bitch don't ever insult me. At least I can see my pussy and touch my toes with ya fat ass, crying to love me having ass. You only mad because I got not one but two of your niggas!" I yelled. pulling Duke behind me.

"Honey I can see my pussy and touch my toes. Meanwhile, you are fucking my ex and my best friend like I'm gonna give you a pass. That's probably ain't his baby either!" she shouted. Ole ummpa loopa ass was mad while I was cheesing. Finally. I had one up that hoe.

"First, I had this man before you and secondly. My baby doesn't concern your bad built body ass so, move the fuck around!" I shouted right back.

"I'm about to kill this hoe!" Fat Ass screamed, attempting to charge me, but Duke pushed her ugly ass back hard.

"The fuck wrong with you? Nigga don't touch her! Juni, get up boo," Nexus screamed, getting pissed.

"I ain't mean that but she ain't about to fight my girl when she about to have my baby."

"You a sorry ass bitch!" Nexus shouted. walking past me and drop kicking her cousin Sia in the face ass Mac came running towards her ass, while Luka and Chance opened the door.

"Nigga I wish the fuck you would. I don't hit my bitch, and I'll be dammed if your punk ass will," Luka based with a scowl on his face. I had to admit though, Demon had some sexy men as friends. Kano hated me from day one, and Luka was too smart and too stuck-up Nexus ass, and Chance, boy he was attractive, but I couldn't take him seriously. Demon was the safest out the three.

"The same way you feel about ya bitch is the same way I feel about mine." Mac gritted.

"See my dude the problem is, I didn't raise my hands to your bitch, but you did to mine. Don't be disrespectful, niggas died for less. Bae, bring your ass over here and sit down for I fuck him up."

Thirty minutes passed, and everyone was still arguing. Fatty was on the phone yelling about the events that took place. Knowing her desperate to be a victim ass, she had to be talking to Demon spilling all the tea that he missed. She made me sick. I hated that bitch. It should have been me to have the supportive mother and loving best friends. I was prettier. So inside. I was torturing myself with envy.

Kano

"Nigga what it do with your ole let's make love looking ass," Devin teased.

I promise, I needed to stop telling that nigga shit because he always teased whenever I showed emotion. I couldn't get my mind off ole girl at Red Lobster. She was gorgeous without even trying. With that smooth skin and sepia eyes, a nigga never had a chance. I wasn't on any forever type shit, but her vibe made me want to know her.

"Nothing much, just getting some work done and shit. Speaking of work. how did that job go?"

“It’s all good. No face no muthafuckin’ case,” he replied before sliding the disk across the desk.

“Good, you got one more job before then you can chill for a while. Did you set things up the way I told you?”

“Yea I did, but I don’t care what you do, make sure baby girl want for nothing. Promise me,” Devin said with conviction, but that came without question.

He had grown so much from the little kid looking for love. We were cutting time close because we were supposed to be meeting at two, but we already had a meeting set up. Before I could ask cuz about the slut bucket he was dating, I heard heels walking on the marble floor.

“JB, you love to make an entrance,” I said, pulling her into a hug, watching the five sexy ass women walking behind her into my office. They all were dressed in form fitted jeans with halter tops and stilettos. They were all beautiful and even though JB was older. her body still looked good as fuck in the clothes they were all wearing.

"That's the only way to do. Boss ass people do boss ass shit. I'd like to introduce you and D to the woman beside the men. This is my sister, Marisol, her daughter, Poetic, and granddaughters Passion, and Kennise, and this is my daughter-in-law, Sunny. These are the faces that you will see if you decide to take the job each week. Here is a folder for you to look over. We are ready to retire and live-in peace and for that to happen death must happen," JB said. Seeing the contents, we were getting paid four million per person.

"You will have to decide which one of you will take the first half of the job and which will do the longer one. You're killing off an organization. We don't have time for mess - ups."

"I'm going to do the six-months job, and Demon is going to do the other."

"That will be a sixty forty split between you two. Kano, you have fifteen people to eliminate. With each kill, the money will be deposited. I cannot stress how time is not on our side and you must cover yourself," the woman. Marisol, said.

“With each kill, the next target gets harder, but you will force them to move the head of the company and that’s where I will be to kill her ass,” JB expressed with so much hatred. I would hate to be on her family’s bad side. You can catch up on them in This *Thug I Love* series.

“The job starts in three months, and Demon you must die as well to protect your family. Can’t kill a ghost because you’re already dead. Oh, and Phantasia is on schedule. Tell the girls to call me for a sit down,” JB said, walking out.

Once we walk them out and locked up, I chatted up with D to see where all his feeling was about this because leaving Juicy was hard for him. I could see the turmoil on his face.

“We can switch if you want,” I suggested. I knew how hard it would be to leave Juniece behind. She was his breath and his peace. Yet he was young and dumb, of course he thought he was protecting her by keeping her at a distance and fucking with that slut bucket.

“Nah I’m good. I’m doing this for my family and the endgame I’m trying to achieve. Enough about this shit. you packed up yet?”

"Shit, nah I went to the gym and showered and threw on a suit for this meeting, but I'm about to change and pack some slight shit for this trip you won't tell where. Just tell me you ain't trying to kill a nigga."

"NIGGGAAA, you get so dramatic every time your birthday comes. Go get dressed.

Handling my hygiene, I went to my dresser and slid on a pair of boxers. After throwing some clothes in my Gucci bag. I opted for some burgundy joggers with me cream and burgundy shirt with my cream Huaraches. So, as I hit the bottom of the stairs, I could hear my cousin going off on the phone with lil' slut bucket. That bitch was an opportunist. and Demon knew that shit. I just wanted him to know real love.

"What's wrong with your ass that you're yelling in my house like you pay bills?" I joked, laughing.

"She went to the house and found out that Nexus and Lyric were coming on the trip and ended up inviting her cousin. Sia, and the nigga Mac. Shit, it's bad enough that fuck nigga

Duke was coming. Then, Luka and Chance said this nigga Duke put his hands on my wife."

"Oh, he must have got a death wish."

"And the cabin left a message saying they gave our cabin to the wrong group and that they will give me a full refund if we take a smaller cabin."

"So how that shit gonna work?"

"I'on even know but you can room with D, since it's both of y'all birthday and we got y'all a master suite."

"Who the fuck is D? I ain't gay or am I rooming with some nigga?"

"Cuz, you know me better than that. D is Juicy's best friend. She grew up with us."

"Then why I never saw her when I would come over? She ugly ain't she?"

"Because your ass stayed in the streets and when you came over after you put me on, she had just left and shit. D. pretty as shit tho. but that's baby sis to me.

"Fuck that if she ugly she's sleeping her ass on the fucking pullout sofa. With a name like D, her ass can probably bench press 280," I said, laughing as we hopped in Devin's truck.

That nigga drove so fast that thirty minutes later, we were pulling up, and everyone was come out. I dapped up my boys, Luka, and Chance. I laughed at them telling me about the fight while the girls were mean mugging the fuck out of Jesscenda. Demon walked over and started beating the shit outta Duke.

"Demon stop, stop it. You ain't got to fight over me," the hoe cried, touching my cousin's cheek.

"Thotisha just working the room, ain't she." Chance joked. holding Lyric ruff rydin ass down.

"Bitch get off me. You thought you was slick. I knew all about you and this nigga. Why you think I stopped fucking you raw. You fuck anybody with money. So why would I be fighting for you. Matter of fact. for ole time's sake I got three stacks if you suck my dick and say the shit you say about that nigga when he not around."

"Bitch, you better not be considering that shit!" Duke managed to yell with blood pouring from his mouth.

"We have to get on the road. Juicy, you are riding with us?" Demon asked, already knowing the answer.

"""Demon, so that's it for us? What about the baby?"

"Call me when you in labor."

"It's probably ain't yours."

"Shut your elephant body ass up. This between me and my man."

"It's funny how you make jokes about me but bothered by little ole me. Why don't I show you why not another bitch will take my place," Juniece said as a matter of fact. She walked up to Devin and palmed his face before feeding him her tongue. After a while. we had to break them up because this grabbed her ass and was about to pick her up like we weren't outside.

"Demon, I hope that fat bitch cheat on you 'cause she ain't as loyal as you think."

"You say slick shit constantly because you are pregnant, hoping nobody gonna fuck you up and not say shit and that is where you are sadly mistaken," Nexus bossed as Luka held her waist.

"Who gonna touch her? Certainly not your ghetto ass!" Sia barked.

"Hoe, you must not know about us because you think you are safe enough to even open your mouth to us. Nobody invited you or your nigga but your hoe ass cousin. Duke punk ass should have stayed home as well cause lawd knows my friend can do wayyyy better than a scrub like you with community dick. How that mouth feel." Lyric made everybody bust out in laughter as Duke stepped forward, only to be stop by Chance.

"This ain't what you want, my nigga, fall back."

"Demon, you going to let them talk to us any type of way?"

"Jessa. you need to chill. You invited your cousin and her nigga for what? At this point. It's not about you. You either going peacefully and shutting the fuck up or stay with your peoples and take a free abortion on me cause the way I feel. I'll shoot all y'all niggas and send flowers to your moms like shit normal."

I was hoping like shit her mannish ass decided to stay because I was planning to enjoy myself for my birthday without looking at her hating ass all weekend.

"Fuck you. Demon. You can have that fat slut. Don't expect me to be waiting for you when you get back!" Jesscenda screamed with Mac, Duke, and Sia hopping in their car and pulling off.

After, a few the girls loaded in one car and the boys loaded in the other. Juicy's friend had a hoodie over her face, so I didn't even see her face. Shit she was probably hiding it 'cause her ass was butt ass ugly. I had wished Drita's fine ass had called me that day. I would have come over that day. I would had made her my birthday present. Two hours later and a mix up about the house we were loading shit in, thank God we stopped at the store so the ladies could cook 'cause a nigga was starving like a muthafucka. I just hope they didn't let Lyric's retarded ass make no food 'cause lawd knows her ass couldn't cook shit. Chance ass was like Mikey; that nigga would eat anything.

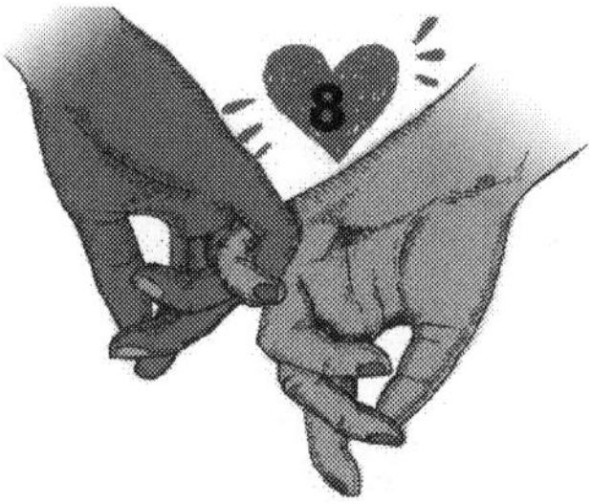

Jesscenda

Bust it down, drink it up
Eat those things that you like
When we love, gave you all of me
I had to learn my place

"Sang that shit, Lyrica, tell that nigga how he makes you feel. Sia, why I ain't good enough for him? Time after time, same ole shit he chooses Fat Albert over me."

"That's your problem, Jess, you worried about the wrong shit. That's Devin's best friend and whether she likes you or not, she still chooses to take the high road when you're on your petty mode. I might don't like Juniece, but I ain't not hater, the girl is pretty as fuck. You don't even want him because you ended up fucking Duke to be spiteful and ended up falling for him, so why not let him be happy and you find your happiness?" my cousin ranted.

"Because I don't want her to win my happiness. Duke is who I want, but I'm with Demon because she's in love with him."

"No matter how much you want to win. things don't always go your way. That man proved today that your time is coming to an end. We lucky 'cause out of our fucked -up family. we got out. Stop thinking like them; everything is not a con. The same way I found my happiness, you can too. Jesscenda."

Sia had a point. For our parents, everything was a con and to walk away for love seemed weak. How can I want something I never knew existed? In my parents' household, making good grades didn't matter; cracking a safe less than two minutes got praise. I lost my virginity at twelve 'cause a con to rob an oil tycoon required it. My age was twelve, but the way my body was built, I could easily go for eighteen. You would think parent who had kids would love them, yet mine couldn't comprehend the meaning I craved of. When Sia fell in love with Mac, she told me to run away with her, and I never looked back.

"Sia, you made it easy to find Mac. What y'all have ain't the easiest, but it's genuine."

"With Mac, I could never waiver. He will always have my loyalty and heart because he would never put me in position to make me feel left out and alone. You're pregnant, Jess, and you have the world at your feet, decide what you want and demand your worth."

"Easy for you to say."

"You are too. Cousin, you are beautiful, it's your attitude that has you fucked- up. Do you and Demon have sex at all?"

"Honestly, bitch, I spend so much of my time trying to keep Fat Ass and Demon away from each other. I find myself begging for his time and energy."

"That right there. When are you going to learn? Baby girl, misery loves company. Duke ain't perfect but loves you. Maybe direct your attention towards someone you don't have to beg to love you."

After talking to Sia, I finished chatting it up and thought about what I really wanted. I was pregnant, and I didn't know who the father was. I called Duke numerous of times and clearly, he was avoiding me. He was mad that I ruined his plans. but so, what? I needed him right now.

Drita

"Even though, I'm good without you, I'm fucking with you regardless
And if that's gon' hurt you, least you can say is I'm honest
Good things don't always get to you the way that you want it"

We sung in sync with Ella Mai as we cooked. The men had yet to come in because they hit up the liquor store. I continued seasoning the meats and throwing them on the indoor grill, smiling and waiting for him to come through the door. I peeped him when I was getting in the truck with the girls, and I wanted this to be a surprise. Even though I told the girls that I knew him and liked him. I couldn't help texting them about the things made me want to give him a chance.

"So tell me if it gets too much
Tell me if you bit too much
Boy, act right 'cause it's cool if
There's too much sauce in the food for you

"So, Drita. how is it that you hooked up but never met?" Lyric's dumb ass asked while making the cranberry, spinach salad. We knew her ass couldn't cook.so this was the safest food to make. I never forgot how we had a potluck, and the bitch tried to poison us all making that bloody ass meatloaf. Nonetheless, that was our girl. He couldn't make us nothing other than salad.

"First. we never hooked up, stupid. He came into my job and left me his number. We texted but still have yet to go out. Don't get me wrong I think he is sexy as shit, but after my history with men, I'm just cautious."

"That still doesn't explain how you two didn't meet until now, especially when he's cousins with your big bro and best friend."

"Between working and keeping my mom outta trouble we never linked up. But just from the little conversations we had. I really like him."

"Well, if you like him, it's a hot girl summer so you might as well be on your bald-headed hoe shit like I'm planning to do with Demon," Juniece crazy ass said. Truth was. I hadn't had sex in well over three years. Kano was the first in years that made me wet from conversation alone.

"I second that motion."

"Drita, you waited this long, bitch a few more won't kill you to make sure he is more than a good lay," Nexus suggested.

"Right, for all I know is his dick could be small as shit."

"It's not," all the girls broke out in unison.

"How the hell do all you bitches know what Kano penis look like?"

"Four years ago, at a pool party, everyone was getting drunk as fuck at this pool party. You didn't come because your boss wouldn't let you get the days off. Anyway. lil daddy drunk way too much Crown because next thing I know, his third leg was swinging off the soft. Shit was so big and thick that thing made its own splash. Any other drink he good, but that Crown be having his ass outta sorts," Juniece explained as we burst out in laughter.

"That's all of them tho. Those fools get real thottie drinking that Crown, that's why I bought a case of it to split, I already put two bottles in each room," Nexus devious behind said. She was always up to something. Fifteen minutes later, the men were walking in while we were setting the table. We had salad, rice with beans, lamb, steak, onion salted homemade bread with peach cobbler that I made personally since I remember Juniece saying it was Kano favorite.

"Damn, y'all did it up for us men," Chance greedy ass said, rubbing his belly.

"Yup, and Drita made peach cobbler," Juniece said, teasing.

"Drita, who?" Kano asked, curious as shit as I stepped forward so he could see me.

"D, Juju's best friend."

"Yea, so you think I'm ugly, huh?"

"Nah, I think that ass fat ass shit and your sexy ass shit wit ya slick ass. The whole time we were in the car, you ain't say shit."

"Slick nah, more like a beautiful surprise. Let's eat then we talk later," I suggested, placing a kiss on his cheek, and grabbing his hand, leading him to the table. Making his plate, I watched him steal glances as he rubbed his hand up and down my thigh.

"Damn, y'all did the damn thing, who made the lamb?" Kano asked.

"We know it wasn't Lyric non-cooking ass. When had dinner at her and Chance's house a few weeks ago, and I almost shot her ass for tryna poison me? I'm somebody's son. Shit, everyone keeps screaming Black Lives Matter, fucking with her I made a whole sign walking around my bedroom. My life matters no more dinners at their house," Luka joked, while we busted out laughing. His ass was dumb as a box of rocks, but he wasn't lying. We all suffered Lyric's cooking wrath at one point or another. Bitch made me meatloaf one time and the shit was still bleeding.

"Shut up, nigga, it was just a little undercooked," Lyric mumbled.

"Little my ass, cuz fighting bitch; you do that shit, styling you dress better than anyone, hold shit down; like no other, but cooking your ass should never do unless it's them Japanese dishes you use to make. You made mash potatoes and that shit was crunchy and suspect as hell." Nexus joked.

"Man, leave my wife alone. Her shit be good," Chance spoke, kissing her on her cheek.

"Oh yea, do Lyric know you be asking Juicy to send you a plate when she cooks, and you eat that shit in the car?" Lyric slaps his ass so quick; the room became cold.

"L, keep them shits to yourself, or we going to have problems, and Demon shut your old snitching ass up nigga." Chance was pissed and so was Lyric, but it didn't even matter. Those fools would have the whole house up because even when they mad. they still fuck and her ass screamed like she was being killed. That's why we did rock, paper, scissors on who was gonna room next to her. Sadly, Nexus lost that battle.

Since we ended up with four rooms, I ended up having to share with Kano. I wasn't mad though. After the dinner was over, we all split into our separate ways. Since our birthdays were a day apart, we ended up with the master suite. I hated clothes when I slept but being around that man had me weak in the knees. I turned the shower on hot to the way I liked it and put my hair in a messy bun. Since I was celebrating my birthday, I wanted to bring it in with a new look. I dyed my hair red and got it straightened bone straight. You couldn't tell me I wasn't the shit. Turning on the music, I started to sing along and shake my ass.

"Ain't no yes-man, but she made him say yeah
She don't need no ring, she so sick of diamonds
Every good girl got a crazy best friend,"

"Oh yeah, Shawty." I looked back only to see Kano grabbing his dick, licking his thick full lips, and watching me twerk my pants off.

"You can't knock?"

"Not when we are sharing the same room," he responded as I fumbled with my bra.

"Let me help you with that and join you in the shower.

"Nah, I'm good."

"Your ass looks like you ain't been fucked right in a while, and I personally think that's a travesty. With a neck this beautiful and an ass that fat, got a nigga ready to bend you over. Why your ass ain't say nothing in the car? I know you saw me."

"Because I wanted to be a surprise. Did you like your surprise?" I turned around, facing him, and wrapping my arms around his neck. His scent was intoxicating that it was sending me over.

"Hell, yeah I did," he responded, lifting me up in the air and wrapping my legs around his waist, carrying me to the shower.

"We ain't having sex."

"Baby girl, your pussy leaking through your drawers. Nipples all hard and anytime I touch you ya body shivers. We are grown as fuck, no judgments no rules. just pain and pleasure. Stop fighting and give in to a menace."

Kano was right; I wanted to be carefree without everyone judging me. I wanted to be fucked so good that I shed tears. My body wanted to feel him, all of him. I wanted him. It's been so long Nexus ass talking 'bout wait she didn't know how hard that would be.

"Tell me what you want, Drita baby, and I promise I'll make that shit happen," he whispered in my ear. He knew what to say to me with all my guards I had up; Kano knocked them down with ease.

"You. All of it. Good, bad, the ugly. Just don't break me. I don't think I can take another heart break."

"You ain't said nothing but a word. Look at me and hear my words, I GOT YOU."

Kano started kissing me and sliding his tongue in my mouth, I relaxed completely like those was meant for me. Sucking on each of my nipples, biting and sucking with the right amount of pressure, putting his hands down my body as I wetted up from his smooth, subtle touches. Kano slid his two fingers inside as his thumb did circular motions on my pussy. I let out a slight moan; not once did Kano lick or suck my clit. Instead, he blew on it to heighten the effect, as I released.

"Ooooh, yes daddy," I moaned out in pleasure.

"Come on, let me taste that cream." That was all I needed to hear as my legs started to shake. Kano licked the sweet nectar oozing out as I leaned my head back, taking it all in.

"Here, taste this," Kano said while gliding his two fingers in my mouth.

I watched him suck all of my juices up. He pushed his long, thick shaft inside me as I gasp for air. Each stoke was a meaning. Knowing what worked and what didn't. it was like we fit. He was going fast and hard, then nice and slow, then circles. It was so good that I had tears dropping. Licking my tears, Kano looked me in the eyes.

"I swear on everything I love, you mine, and I'll forever be yours." Kissing me hard, and grabbing my neck, Kano stared into my eyes as we released together.

Damn, I'm in trouble. Dick so good make you wanna marry him. I sang in my head.

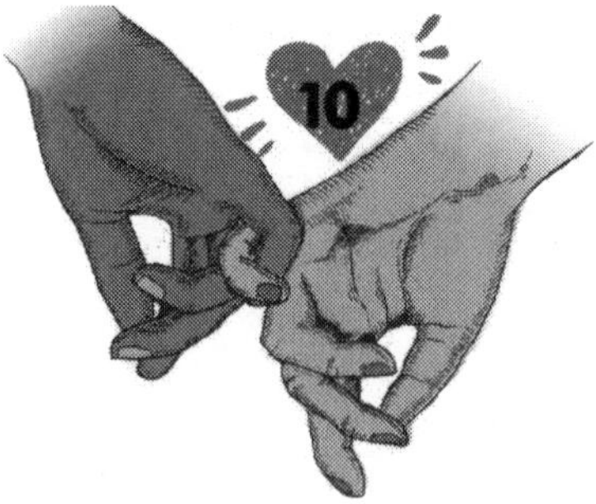

Lyric

I was sitting on the side of the bed lowkey heated that my own nigga was out in these streets eating other bitches' meals like I couldn't cook. I'on even care that the bitches were my friends because they always said my ass couldn't cook, but I never believe them because my nigga would hype me up, so of course I was going with bae's words. but his big-headed ass wasn't even loyal by lying to me. Even my momma said her, and her dogs wouldn't eat the food I cook, and she ate potted meat sandwiches. But let's be clear, I could cook the fuck outta Ramen dishes. It was soul food that gave me issues. My first job was at a Japanese eatery, so you tend to eat what you know. However. Chance hated Japanese food, so I tried to cook things his selfish ass would love. He always said when you learn to infuse it with cannabis, let him know.

"Ly baby, I know your ass ain't mad 'cause I ate a few meals. You know Juni can throw down better than my momma," Chance said, soaking wet with a towel around his waist, staring me down. The nigga looked so good that my mouth watered thinking about putting Chance's long, thick shaft in my mouth.

"I don't care if your petty ass told me the truth, I could have taken classes, bought cookbooks, followed recipes, but no when you hyped me up so good that when the church bake-off always came, I'd enter. No wonder Sister Patterson suggest I should buy store bought desserts," I ranted.

"Sister Patterson needs to not talk; bitch can barely cook her damn self. Bae, you know I hate to hurt your feelings. What's really going on because you already knew your ass couldn't cook, so tell me what's been bothering you," Chance asked, cupping my chin.

"The girls and I was talking about the next chapter in our lives, and everyone had a plan. Juniece going to college for business management, Nexus is already in college with plans of opening an investment firm, Drita drew up a whole business venture with Juniece and enrolled in college, but me. I have nothing."

"We good, though. We got bread, and we not hurting for shit," Chance said.

"That's it though. That is your hard-earned money not mine."

"Go ahead with all that shit. Lyric. Not once have I ever told you can't spend or touch my accounts. Hell, your name on every fucking thing I got. So again, what is all this about?"

"I applied for and internship and it's for two years in Hokkaido. Chance, I love you so much, baby, but I need to do this, and I want to do this for me. I want to stand next to my friends and be able to be proud of myself. My parents weren't shit. When we have a son or daughter. I want them to see their mom worked hard for them so they should do the same."

"So, you were going to leave me, huh? But to be honest, Ly, all those women I flirted with could never say they fucked me or sucked my dick since we been together."

"It's still disrespectful as fuck. You friendly as fuck, and I hate it even knowing what I know about us. I still get jealous because niggas leave, men leave, so every day I think that girl is the girl who's going to make him leave. I can't cook, some days I am confident, other days struggle. so yea I was going to leave because I'm not in the business of keeping niggas who don't want to be kept. Staying around beating bitch's ass and looking stupid was nowhere in my plan. Then, you got your shit together and started doing right. So, I asked myself to choose you or accomplish my dreams?"

"When I met you, I couldn't stop staring. You looked sad even though your cousin was standing right beside you. It took you almost three months to even say hi back to a nigga. I thought you was weird as shit. We finally hit that stride though becoming best friends and turned into my girlfriend. The way you love me scared me. Before you, I didn't exist without you, I might as well kill myself. We young as fuck, but there not a woman who can do for me like you do. Ly baby."

"And what do I do for you?"

"You know my secrets, and when my world is crashing, and I need to let it all go, you find a way to ground me. When do you gotta be there?"

"In three months, it comes with an allotment and an apartment."

"Yo, why would I care what the fuck it comes with, Lyric? I know your slick ass too damn well. So, speak that shit."

"We both know if I go to Japan, and you stay here we're not going to make it, and I can't take you hurting me again. I swear, I love you so let's make the most of what we have here and part, and if the time comes again, we should try to pick up where we left off," I said just above a whisper.

A lot of people always wondered why I stayed with Chance all these years, but he always had potential. He wanted love but didn't know how to love me, so I taught him. I wanted to be treated rough in the bedroom and loved throughout the bad times. I desired his touch. We became one and like I breathe, I needed him as he need me so know this shit was hard as fuck. Ms. Brooke knew about everything and told me to follow my heart and don't hide nothing. If he was right for me, the answer would be simple. He'd choose me and wouldn't let go.

For the first ten minutes, Chance never said anything. The look on his face told it all. Instead, he dropped his towel on the floor came over to me, grabbed me by my ponytail, and moved his thick ten-inch masterpiece to my face. Opening my mouth, I swallowed him whole. I sucked the tip, swirling my tongue and massaged his balls in my hands.

"Lyric, don't fuckin' play with me, do that shit right!" Chance barked. I spit on his shaft and deep throated his dick like I whirlwind of water was incasing it as a massage. Picking up the pace as this man fucked my face 'til he came and like he taught me, I swallowed every drop like a mere dog begging for a treat.

"Assume position four."

He walked over to the dresser as I was lifted on top with my legs wide open. Feeling his tongue had me screaming so loud that Nexus was banging and screaming, but it couldn't be helped, good dick was hard to find. He flickered his tongue back and forth with tears filling my eyelids. With Chance, sex was euphoria; only he could do this to my body without remorse. Standing up, Chance guided his dick in me nice and hard, pounding me relentlessly.

"Fuckkkkk," I shouted damn near slobbering at the mouth. Licking the slobber on my chin and force feeding me his tongue sent me overboard.

"Now say all that shit was talking about leaving me," Chance gritted, grabbing my neck as I continued to moan loud as fuck.

"Can't speak? Well, listen wherever you go, I go. We are one. There's not ever an out to this so as long as I got breath in my, we will always be. EVEN IN MUTHAFUCKIN JAPAN." He pounded me harder and harder as tears began to fall. I tell you this man was my weakness, and I was his. We understood when others didn't. We continued to fuck through our differences for the remainder of the night. This man was so damn dope. Truth is the day I met Chance was the day I found myself.

Nexus

"I swear to God, Chance, and Lyric. I wanna sleep got dammit. Y'all fuck way too much. Bitch should have a yeast infection!" I screamed through the walls. These fools went from arguing to fucking in a matter of minutes. I was tired as hell. Luka had already gone to sleep in the van because he said that he wasn't tryna be questioned by the cops when his heart stop after fucking my cousin.

"Oh, nah don't be scared. Take all this shit!" Chance screamed through the walls. I swear them bitches set me up, they knew I couldn't play rock, paper, scissors. Grabbing my robe, I went to the kitchen to see

Juni and D, sharing a plate of peach cobblers and ice cream.

"I swear to God ya cousin really needs to go to rehab for that sex life of hers," Juicy said, mad as hell. As a she attempted to wash her hands, Devin stopped her by sucking on each of her fingers.

"Bro, I ain't know you got game like that. I see you cat daddy," I hyped him up.

"Yo, who the fucks say that. You are being a whole creep."

"Yassss I'mma creep and you freak, I'mma creep, I'mma creep, and you freak.," I sang as them two busted out laughing while twerking.

"Where Drita at?"

"Getting that ass waxed. Why you think we up. Those fools just as loud as the 2 Live Crew upstairs." She giggled.

"How it is going between you two," I tried to whisper.

"Her nasty ass keeps tryna take my goodies and shit but enough of all that, Juicy, I'm hungry."

"D, there's food in the fridge. Want me to make you a plate?" Juniece's crazy ass said, not picking up the seduction in his voice.

"I ain't talking about that food. The food I want," Demon said the rest in her ear that had her blushing.

Her ass ran out the kitchen with Demon running behind her, smacking on her ass. I was so happy for my girl; she spent so many years loving him in secret which hurt us to see her in pain. I got it though, everybody went to the same middle school except Kano, so we were all close. Our grandma ended up raising Lyric and I until we were eleven. When our grandma, Mae, died, her friend from our church took us in. Chance's mom. Brooke, raised us and then we met the boys, and I met my little silent killer, Luka. He never said much just watched how people move. Everyone called him One - Hitta-Quitter 'cause if you fought him, one punch would knock ya ass smooth right out. Heating me up two lambchops, I crushed them instantly then cleaned up my mess. Instead, of staying in the house, I went climb in the truck because there was no way I was going to get any sleep otherwise. At least, I didn't have to hear them fucking and screaming all night. This was the worst time to be on my period.

"What took you so long, Stinka?"

"Eating some leftovers."

"Greedy ass. Gimme kiss and come get some sleep," Luka demanded.

Even in the dim light, you could see his rich, smooth chocolate skin and deep, brown eyes with dimples to match. This man was mine. Climbing on his lap, I granted his request and kissed him then laid on his chest. Throwing the blanket over us, we fell asleep.

****

6 a.m.

I woke up having to pee so damn bad, soon as I started to move, Luka tightened his grip around my waist while using the other hand to grab my ass cheek. Lawd knows I couldn't hold it, and I didn't want to wake him up but shit if I stayed here, I would have for sure marked Luka with my piss.

"Babe, I gotta pee," I whispered, wiggling in his arms.

"Are you coming back?" he managed to ask.

"No, we have to get breakfast started, so I'mma shower and get dressed. You are coming up?"

"Yea, the 2 Live Crew should be asleep by now."

After picking through my clothes, I opted for peach, high -waisted jeans with a white and peach halter top. Then, showered until I was satisfied. I pat myself dry and oiled my body as my ringtone for people who wasn't saved in in my phone went off.

"Hello," I replied as I picked up on the third ring.

"Yes, can I speak to Nexus Grant?"

"This is her; how can I help you?"

"I'm a case worker with the department of social services. I have Nala and Nate Grant in custody, and you are listed as next of kin."

"I'm sorry you have the wrong number. I don't know a Nala or Nate."

"Your mother is Anissa Grant, correct? Born August 22, 1966?"

"Yes, but I haven't seen her so I can't help you."

"Ma'am, she passed two days ago from breast cancer, and your younger brother and sister is here with me, and you're listed as the next of kin."

"Me and my mother was estranged and that's putting it lightly. Where is their father?"

"Incarcerated, he gave up his rights when the kids were born. If I'm being honest, Ms. Grant, if you don't take them, your siblings will be split up and as much as I hate to say, it too many things happen to kids in the system, and we're overcrowded and overworked as is. Your mother left a letter in case anything should happen to her."

"Look, I'll be on vacation for another five days. Is there a way you can' text me all the info, and I'll come to you, and we can go from there?"

"That will work, see you soon."

This was always like my mother pulling some tired ass stunt. She died doing what she did best, being fucking selfish and not giving me the chance to say fuck you or see you later. She never cared to meet me or to build a relationship with me, but she gave that to her other kids. I was furious and sad. Why wasn't I good enough? What did I do that I wasn't good enough for her to stay? The next chapter of my life didn't require fucking kids. Hell. I was still a kid myself and telling Luka had me scared shitless. Deciding not to spend too much time on it, I finish preparing for the day.

Demon

Looking at Juicy, she made my world right. I never even thought that taking a chance on this would feel this good. On a ride to the cabin, we all talked about our girls, and we realize as unlucky as all of our lives have been, God saw fit to grace with the women we needed most. I struggled so hard thinking if I could leave her in three months, truth was, I was ready to give it all up, but at the same time this was a chance of a lifetime, so she had to be able to endure the pain that I was about to put her through. Truthfully, I owed Drita an apology. When she told me how much of a snake Jesscenda was; I didn't listen. Maybe the back of my mind always knew, that's why this opportunity didn't really fuck with me like that or maybe she did, I just didn't care. I wanted these next few months to be filled with memories to cherish.

"I love you, juicy booty," I whispered in her ear. Since I tasted her sweet peach, I been hooked. That nickname I called her fit just right.

"I love you too, Demon."

"You mean that or you just trying to hype a nigga up for the D?"

"I've been real with you since day one, my love for you runs past lifetimes."

"So, I leave this world tomorrow what would you ask me to leave you? Money? House? Car?"

"No, I could never ask you to leave me any of those things. See if I'm being real, I loved you the moment I met you and if you leave here tomorrow, I want a piece of you that's going to last that shows our love that embraces our endurance because that's what our love does, endure.

"You stand by that?"

"A million percent," Juicy responded. I moved my dreads out my face. "After we graduate, I want to go to college for two years and get a loan for a mini strip mall with stores that offer the ultimate experience like one store some type of gym that offers classes and serves dietary, yet healthy meals, and maybe a soul food place. Who knows, the possibilities are endless."

"You can do it. I always believed in you."

"What do you want to do after graduation?"

"Haven't thought about it. People tried to count me out, but you and ma dukes never gave up on me. Whatever my future holds, know I want it to include you," I replied, turning over, lighting the blunt I rolled earlier in the day. Tomorrow, I had planned a night away from the cabin for Juicy and I. her freaky ass kept on wanting me to fuck her. but the way I see it, she deserved to be worshipped.

"And if a nigga breaks your heart, can you ever forgive him?"

"No but if you break my heart, your ass damn sure better come and repair it."

"Bet." That was all that needed to be said. For the remainder of the night, Juniece and I talk like we use to all night. Laughing and joking like we did a few weeks ago before all our real feelings came into play.

"Devin?"

"Yeah."

"I don't want no special drawn out plan to lose my virginity. Right now, I just want you."

She pulled my long shirt. She wore over her head revealing her curvaceous, beautiful, sculpted body. She ran her hand through her long curly hair, pushing it to one side and climbed on my lap. She smoothly traced my lips with her tongue before sticking it in my mouth.

"I don't want you to regret nothing," I said just above a whisper in between our kisses as I gripped her waist.

"Here's what I regret, not telling you my feelings long ago and allowing lil Jezebel to come in and touch what's mine. I regret not being the first to sit on this big ass dick as it eases inside me but now, I chose to do this. Because I feel like even though you're right here, I can't help but feel your mind is far away."

Placing subtle kiss on her collarbone, touching every part of her body, etching it into my mind seeing what parts made her moan. Picking Juicy up, I laid her on the king size bed. I kissed on her thighs, staring at her perfectly shaved pussy as if it was crafted for me. Diving headfirst, that nickname suited her perfect as her wetness leak out.

I slid a finger in and kept rotating between my mouth and my finger sending her into a frenzy.

"Umm don't stop," Juniece moaned between shallow breathes.

"I got you, Juicy booty." After she came two more times, I placed my dick at her entrance as her eyes bucked wide as fuck. I got it tho, I was well endowed. On a soft, I was a good ten and half in inches. On a hard, I was damn near twelve, but I wouldn't hurt her. If anything, I wanted to make her feel wanted. I needed to imprint my love on her pussy and her heart so deep that she never doubted her worth. I eased in as a tear fell out her eye as I kissed it away.

"Juicy, it's only gon hurt a little I'mma push the rest in." I pumped slowly, watching all the faces as I pleasured her relentlessly.

"Devin, don't ever leave me!" she screamed out in pleasure. "Promise me."

"I promise, baby, I will never leave you intentionally." For hours on end, Juniece and I made love in this room doing everything under the sun.

I taught her how to please me, and she did the same. Four hours later, I was holding Juicy like I never wanted to let her go while smoking a blunt, letting my playlist fill the room. Then heaven played throughout the room and for the first time in my life, I started singing to someone other than myself.

"You asked a question and I, ain't gonna lie

But, I wasn't ready still you took me by surprise

You wanna know if I will, ever leave your side

But I will love you till the very day I die

Girl, I need you I've been needing you like air

Don't know how I would survive without you dear

I could scream it loud for the whole world to hear

And if they call me crazy, I don't care

"That song is so beautiful, babe. And why didn't I know you could sing?"

"Yeah Banky, wrote it for his wife Su Su when he wanted to propose. The moment I heard it, it reminded me of you."

"Well, I don't care if it's on heaven or earth. I still want to be beside you."

"I feel the same way Juicy booty."

Duke

"Ahhh, fuckkk!" Jesscenda screamed while I dug deep in her guts. Her arms wrapped around my body while her teeth seeped deep into my neck. "Don't stop! Please don't stop!" she continued.

Using my hand, I gripped her neck and gently squeezed as her pussy muscles contracted around my dick. Sex with Jesscenda was always immaculate because she knew how to please me. She was submissive to the dick, and she abided by whatever rules I gave her.

"Squeeze that dick!" I demanded lowly in her ear, slowly dipping the tip of my shit into her moist pussy. Pregnant pussy was the best pussy and my shit drowned in Jesscenda's.

"Oh God! I'm about to"

Lips curled, eyes rolling towards the back, her legs shook with no mercy as she released a breath of relief. Following suit, I leaned down and gently bit her on her neck. Flipping her over, I laid across her back and landed kisses down her spine.

In a perfect world, I could have been with her, but she came with too much baggage and knowing that she was with that bitch ass nigga. Demon, caused me to keep my feelings for her at bay. I loved Jesscenda. We had history, and she had looked out for me when I was too stubborn to look out for myself.

Swinging her legs over she got up and ran her fingers through her hair as her phone started to blare on my nightstand.

"Shit!" She jumped up and started grabbing her clothes.

"Yo, you seriously rushing to get back to that nigga!" I snapped before I could stop myself. I knew what it was between us, but the fact that she was possibly carrying my seed had changed any hesitance I possessed when it came to checking her.

"He's—"

"Answer it!" I told her, blowing smoke from the blunt I had just lit, and her eyes bucked.

"Wh... what?" she stuttered. "I'm not doing that," she responded, pulling her shirt over her head.

I was pissed because the nigga hung up and called right back. Demon was a cocky nigga and he thought he was the shit because he was eating better than I was. Not to mention that he had the woman I wanted. Knowing that Jesscenda's kid could possibly be his caused rage to soar through me.

"Answer the phone or I will!" I sneered, grilling her.

"Are you really doing this right"

My head tilted. She was pissing me off. I jumped up from the bed and made my way towards the nightstand and she quickly snatched up her phone, answering it.

Demon had recently found out that I had been smashing his girl, but it didn't move me. I had those same feelings he did when it came to the woman standing in front of me.

"Hey"

"Why the fuck you not answering the phone?" his voice erupted through the phone and her eyes shot towards me. My jaws flexed before I bit my bottom lip, grilling her.

When it came to Jesscenda, I learned how to appreciate a woman. I learned the likes and dislikes of a woman and was cautious with it. Yet that didn't mean that I would allow her to play me along with another nigga.

"What are you"

"Don't fucking play with me, Jessa, I know you over there with that nigga. I would have never thought my shorty was a hoe. Hoe ass probably pregnant by that nigga."

I grilled the phone then looked at her. As I prepared to respond her hand flew up against my mouth while her eyes pleaded with me not to say shit. She loved him and that ripped open a wound I thought I had closed long ago.

It burned me up that she was trying to protect his feelings all the while stepping on mine. Before I realized it. I went off.

"Get the fuck out!" I roared as she clenched the phone with her hand over the mic so he couldn't hear me.

"Duke please!" she pleaded while I tossed the rest of her shit at her.

It didn't matter that she was his. She was mine too. We had built this bond and to see that it was all a lie had me wanting to kill her right where she stood.

"What that nigga say?" Demon questioned. "I'm telling you Cenda. Tell that"—"

"Nah, nigga you tell me!" I huffed with my chest out. Demon's money was way longer, and he had a fool ass army by his side, yet I wanted war. I wanted him to understand that I wasn't leaving that easily.

"When I see yo' bitch ass it's up!" He ended the call, and she proceeded to start crying. I didn't give a fuck. I was tired of her thinking she could play us both. The shit was lame.

"Why would you do that, Duke?" Jesscenda had the nerve to question.

"Fuck that! You just finished fucking and sucking on me and soon as your nigga call you want to run to him. I'm sick of that shit."

I sat on the bed with my head in my hands thinking about how all this shit had gone on. I had found myself entangled in Jesscenda's web of lies and I wanted out. I wanted to go back to how it all was before but knowing that she was pregnant had caused a halt to everything.

"You knew that I was with—"

"Get the fuck out!" I roared louder seeing that she hadn't heard me the first time. I was over playing this game with her and that nigga because she would never fully be mine, and I couldn't come to grasps with that.

Shaking her head, she wiped her face and picked up her shoes from the floor. Her head hung low as if she was defeated as she walked towards the door. I was done. At least that's what my mind was saying, yet my heart knew the truth. Dating Juniece was something like a pass time to make Cenda Jealous, but a blind man could see when it came to that she wasn't nowhere on par with my baby. after taking a quick shower and getting dressed, I left to meet up with my Garrett who everyone referred to as ally boy. He was smoking a fat ass blunt with Mac as I walked in and crashed my root into a seat kicking it across the floor.

"Nigga, who shit in your Cheerios?"

"You already know who it is." I replied through clenched teeth.

"You keep giving that hoe too much power. She might love you but Jesscenda envy that niggas bank roll. I got ya back a hundred grand but going to war over a female where money rules everything around her, ain't smart."

Ally Boy was right. We loved each other but fighting for Jesscenda when I wasn't sure she'd pick me was foreign as fuck. I needed to figure out this shit quick because I was slowly losing my mind.

Luka

"My turn my turn. Devin, what was it about your girl that made you chase her, and sex cannot be the answer." Juniece said reading the card from game night sipping on her wine as Devin's ole whipped ass spoke first. We had been playing everything from spades, dice, to family feud and now this damn couple game the women created.

"For me it was the moment she called me mean with her lip curled up and her hands on her hip. The earth stood still. She was cute and stood up to me with all the confidence in the world until she realized I was checking her out."

"Really bae, aww." Juniece gushed as she got up. sliding her tongue in Devin's mouth.

"Soft ass niggas man," Chance stupid ass had a nerve to say like we didn't know all the shit he did for crazy Lyric's ass.

"Nigga!"!" all the men yelled out shocked. See

chance was a special case when it came to Lyric and vice versa. That's why they always had to have at least one couple as a witness to their bullshit.

"Senior prom Lyric and you was at odds and ends up going with that fool Cash and you got so mad that you knocked ole boy out when they were dancing, and you carried her home only to lock her in a closet until she told you she loved you again."

"Shit worked tho. She told me she was with me 'til the end and just like Chucky it ain't the fucking end 'til I say so," that fool replied as we all busted out laughing because everyone knew he was serious.

"I swear Chance next lifetime…."

"You still gon be with me, cause this dick said so," Chance cut Lyric ass off kissing her ass stupid. We played for a few more rounds while joking laughing and drinking. After we was done since it was men's turn to cook, we grilled ribs, chicken, and shrimp. Then I made potato salad with some stir fry vegetables like my momma taught me. Joking, smoking, and laughing with my friends thinking how I changed yet remained the same.

Growing up in a Nigerian and Black household there was never a dull moment. I admired the love my father had for my mother and appreciated the fact that he only chose to make her a wife... Dola Musa first time seeing my mom was magical as he says but, the truth was in the dark, we were so far from perfect as we thought. Unbeknownst to my mother, my father had four other wives and ten other children. She asked him to choose, and he refused to change. My mother was a lot of things, but a fool she wasn't. Lee'Andra Musa walked away from her marriage of ten years and her husband without shedding a single tear and I remember asking her "why leave without fighting and saying your peace? Are you not angry?"

She turned to me and stared at me for the first time during the whole ordeal happened. "In life, some things are not worth forgiving. See I can forgive a lot of things, but I won't forgive his deception. He expected me to be bitter, hurt, and angry, he wanted me to shout at him. and he didn't deserve to hear my feelings. Remember this. my son words and deception can hurt people. If you speak make sure it's something that needs to be said instead of meaningless notions." Those words stuck with, so I watched and listed. Never said much unless I had something worth saying. It wasn't until I met Nexus and others learned to walk in faith and stand by my principles, bask in my truth, and cherish the family I built.

"Babe you, okay?" Nexus asked, bringing me out my thoughts.

"Yea I'm good, beautiful." After the game finished, it was time for the couples' talent show. Now I'd like to say our talent show had a lot of talent, but I'd be lying if I said there wasn't a reason, we were all friends. We laughed, cried, and went through shit together even if it meant embarrassing ourselves in the process. First up was Ike and Tina with all the get up.

"Anna Mae get on out here girl!" Chance yelled with this afro wig playing the guitar holding his mic in a tan suit with a pic sticking out his head.

"Anna Mae, you hear me girl," Chance called Lyric ass pretended to trip before grabbing the mic.

"Rock me, baby, rock me all night long. I said I want you to rock me baby, rock me all night long."

They had all of us buss out laughing as they were damn near twerking. I couldn't wait for they ass to be done. Then. Drita and Kano came out rapping Ying Yang Twins and didn't know none of the damn lyrics. but hey lil shawty let me whisper in your ear. Juniece and Demon ass took the cake because these niggas was up in here singing songs from Rent. so, about time it was Nexus and I's turn. we just sung the Boondocks theme song. Bout time everyone was done. it was three in the damn morning, and no one could pick a damn winner.

Now I don't know about everyone else, but I knew my girl and although she was having fun, she was tired and worried about something. When we got in our room, Nexus sat on the bed staring off in space and remained quiet. Lifting her up I placed her on my lap and ran my hand through her hair laying her in my chest, never saying anything. Nexus busted out crying.

"When I was little, I use to dream that my parents would come back and give me this noble reason for living with my Big Momma instead of the truth. I heard stories about my momma, but I always thought I get the chance to tell her I felt. How I did okay without her. Today I got a call saying she passed, and I have two younger siblings that was left to me, Nexus managed to say through her tears wetting up my shirt. I kept consoling her as she continued to cry instead of responding. "Their twins, and I have so much anger towards them. What was special about them that she raised them and not me? Why would she leave them kids with me?"

"Babe, you have every right to feel how you feel. That woman scared you in ways I can't understand and then had the audacity to ask you to raise the kids she chose to bring in this world. That is fucked up and if you choose to walk away, I got you. In the same token they are your siblings. Can you really walk away without wanting to know anything?

"I don't know. All I do know is that I'm angry. Does that make me a bad person?"

"Not at all."

"I'm a kid too. I'm only nineteen and in college. You take care of me. I can't expect you to just take on two more burdens on the strength of me." Nexus replied as I gave her this confused ass look. Her as think she's slick. All the girls were though.

"Nah don't use that shit as in excuse. Don't make me and our finances the reason you walk away from your siblings. If you do that it's fine, it's your choice, but ya ass know we damn sure well off. Plus, we have that house with all of them empty rooms. You're their sister not their mother," I scolded her.

Chance, Kano, Devin, and I all worked for JB. However, I came from money and chose not to use my father's money. At twenty years old, I was a very successful man. This clearing house job we been doing left us rich. not even counting the money we did since we were young as fuck killing like that shit was natural. I think our motivation for each of us was independence. None of us wanted to ask another muthafucka for anything again.

"You're right, and I'm curious about them, but bae I can't say I still want to take them in, but I do want to meet them."

"Okay, baby girl. Since we were going home tomorrow anyway, let's pack and take a cab to the airport, and we can go from there."

"Yeah, I can do that."

"I have to have this meeting with the boys really quick, and we can head out."

"That's fine. I want to tell the girls everything as well too." Nexus replied, getting off my lap. Getting myself together, I walked in the movie room we used as a man cave.

"Nigga, the meeting started an hour ago. What you and Nexus upstairs doing, fucking?" Kano asked.

"Shit, I wish," I replied, making me a drink. I poured a glass of Henny to the brim and downed it.

"Luka, wassup!" Demon roared. Whenever you looked at him, he looked like an ordinary ass nigga with a bitch feature but had this deep baritone that commanded the room. We all joked about his ass being that he was the youngest.

"Cutie calm down," I joked, calling him by his nickname.

"Stop calling me that shit. It's not my fault my mom features were stronger wit yo ugly ass." We all busted out laughing.

"For real though we are leaving tonight."

"For what we are checking out tomorrow?" Kano replied rolling a fat ass blunt in the recliner.

"Nexus found out her mother died and had two other kids, and the only one who can take care of them is her. So, we have to meet with the case worker in the morning."

"She gon take them, or no?" Kano asked.

"She not sure, we going to meet them and decide after that."

"How you feel about this?"

"Man D, that woman is everything to me and knowing how she feel about her mom, I know this is the hardest shit she's been through. They're her siblings. If she take 'em, cool, we got the space, and if we don't I know she gon regret that shit because she don't want anyone to feel like she did when she found out parents didn't want her." I replied. Inhaling the blunt kept me cool. Nexus wore her heart on her sleeve.

"Damn bruh, my girl petty ass upstairs telling her to leave them krusty ass kids in there!" Chance yelled out as we busted out laughing. He was a fool because Lyric didn't give a fuck and said that same shit. Sitting straight up. we all knew that this conversation needed to be had.

"Demon, we all agreed were going to walk away with the money we have and tell JB to find someone else, that way you won't leave Juniece," I said in a low but stern tone.

"Funny because last time I checked, I was a grown ass man, and I made the choice to do this. We had a plan."

"The plan didn't require you dating and leaving Juicy. We made more than enough money, bro," Chance argued.

But that only infuriated Devin. For Devin to be the youngest, he was our leader and telling him what to do was like spitting in your face. We might have been older, but he had this dream that we all wanted to achieve. It was little after D's parents died, and we completed our first job for JB as we sat in the room with ten thousand each. While everyone was thinking how to blow their cash, Devin was thinking about a bigger picture.

"D, what's going on, bruh?"

"Y'all, I was thinking how we got to make some money and it's good. Where y'all see yourselves in the next five, ten years? Luka, you're not broke but you are prideful. You hate having to spend your daddy's money

and you hate having to ask your mom for shit, so you work. Chance, your mom workday in and day out providing for you and the girls working a dead-end job. Kano we all know auntie story and you all know mine."

"What are you getting at?" I yelled out.

"That don't y'all want to never have to worry about a dollar ever again and be your own boss?" We all nodded. "Me too. Me and Ma sit back and talk about plans. We smart, but I got a plan that I wanna achieve and if you trust me by the end of the year, I'll make you millionaires. But give me fifteen years, and I'll make sure we have generational wealth money."

"How?"

"Well, first I want to start Phantasia Incorporated. The board members will be Kano, Chance, Luka, and I and each of us put up fifty g's per person. If we are making ten g's for these small bounties imagine how much we can make for the big ones. That means we need to be the team that need to work to the top. Also, we will put up money for the girls that are true blue because if anything happens to us, they can be good regardless. I got Juicy and a childhood friend of ours. I also would like to add Ms. Lee, Ms. Julissa, and Ms. Brooke, who I already talked to and already have their money aside."

"Cuz, she solid?"

"K, I wouldn't mention her unless I trusted her like each of you."

"Say less. Then I got her share."

"Bet."

"I got Ly Baby."

"And I got Nexus, but why are you having our mothers on the board."

"Chance, your mom is a real estate agent, Ms. Julissa is a financial advisor, and Ms. Lee is a designer. We need them for the next phases, there's this land that's attached to a strip mall that's between Culper and Brandywine. We are going to buy it with the money that we put up and continue to every quarter make payments. Lee, Julissa, and Brooke agreed to work under our company each having a department for their field. We will need an accountant until you finish your degree. Nothing will be illegal, but I still want his ass to know the bare minimum."

"When you talked to our mothers?" Chance said through clenched teeth.

"Like I said, me and Ma spent plenty of nights talking feeding off each other ideas. It helped me not think about losing my mom, so I asked her was my idea possible, and she called Lee and Brooke; for months they helped refine the plan. Back to what I was saying, we will smartly invest using Phantasia incorporated for keeping and buying property. Right now, it's a steal. No one wants the hassle of trash land because it can take a fortune to repair it, but I know the potential and when

we buy all of it, we will open shops for the money to flow in. Watch your woman motivate them, inspire them so when the time comes, they know how to quadruple our money. With the land part with sixty percent of it, Ms. Brooke, and Ms. Lee gon build estates and then auction off and making a gated community offering an exclusive experience. And the other forty percent we will build our gated utopia. The women will be in the dark until after college. That's the dream, are you still in?"

That day, we all agreed to follow Devin's young ass, and he hadn't failed us yet. We lived modest for the most part and we were all in college, going to college, or about to graduate with degrees. Then, JB came to us about this billion-dollar job, and we hopped on. All the money we made for this job was being transferred into a Swiss bank account, and when it's done, we split evenly.

"Y'all know Juicy my baby, but the plan hasn't changed ."

"And what if she can't forgive you or what if she tries to kill herself? Money ain't everything, D, we ain't hurting for money."

"Kano, I'll deal with that when the time comes, but you keep her safe until I get back. Y'all my brothers, and I'm sorry for the burdens I'm asking you to do, but I will do this JOB!" Devin yelled.

"We got you, baby bro," we all said in unison. To be Black men in a world where we are constantly doubted, it felt good to know our hard work was all worth it. We chopped it up for a few more and went our separate ways. Trust the plan, that's what all this is for.

Kano

"Aye cuz before you go to sleep. Remember when you put up for our friend for the board?"

"Yea, you gon tell me who she is?"

"Drita, I see the vibe. Lay the foundation and build on that shit, big nigga." he preached before I went in the room.

I was glad though. After she told me about her childhood, I wanted nothing but to see her win. Whether she chose to stay with me or not, but I wanted to give this a shot. Like the promise my cousin made we was making more money than we could count, I was finishing up my degree in accounting and business management, while majoring in computer technologies, and Luka studied law. Ever since we heard his dream, each of us promised to always follow and respect one another.

"Hey, baby?" Drita said before kissing me on my lips.

I know a lot feel like I should take things slower, but shit I can't even lie, I wanted what everybody had. Someone who I could tell my problems to and joke and lay around the house and have dinner ready when I got home. The late-night conversations told me everything, and I couldn't stop wanting to be in her space.

"Hey, lil mama. You smell all fresh and shit."

"That's because I just showered. After talking with the girls, I realized that I want to cuddle and spend a little time just us before we go back to reality."

"What you mean?"

"I mean this past couple of days has been nice and truthfully, I'm scared that once we get home you are going fear that you got what you want so what left," Drita whispered, shocking the fuck outta me. I wasn't surprised though a blind man could tell she had trust issues.

"Come on and sit on my lap."

Doing as she was told Drita climbed on my lap and wrapped her arms around my neck, staring me in her eyes with her lips poked out. I just couldn't resist and leaned in kissing her as a soft subtle moan escaped her mouth.

"Drita, you're guarded as fuck man, and the dude that made you this way makes me want to beat his ass and thank him in the same breath. He didn't know your worth, but I do. Lil mama, I ain't never had a girl. Most times, we fucked and on to the next. No girl made me want to cuff them until I met you. I'm not perfect, I'm new to this, and I'm going to mess up, but if you honestly give us a chance, I promise to give you everything you desire, and I ain't talkin' bout that material shit either because you'll get that for yourself. I'm talking about speaking life into your soul and restoring your once broken heart, being your peace inside the madness, this I can do for you and this I will do for us."

"What if later you feel you aren't ready?"

"What if I become the best for you there ever was?" Drita pondered on the words I spoke and took a deep breath. "I'm yours."

Since Drita decided to trust me with her heart, I decided to do the same in return. I told her what I did for a living. I expected her to say she couldn't deal with being a killer came with, which I couldn't blame her. Instead, she asked me is being a killer my end game. When I replied no, she said long as I protected her, she would do the same. We didn't rush what we were building. I instead, we agreed to date exclusively, and she would come work as my assistant while attending college and figuring out what she wanted to do after that.

I never thought I needed love until I saw what it could do. The late-night conversations to the jokes to the sexual attraction we had towards each other only pulled me closer towards her. I needed her, and the more time we spent together the more I was convinced that woman was perfectly crafted for me.

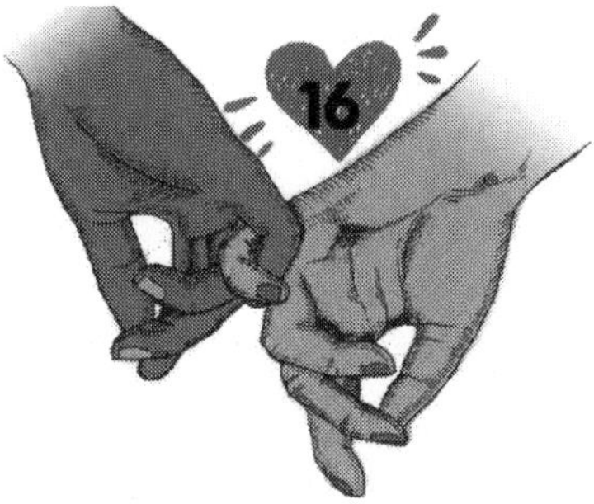

Nexus

I was standing outside social services, and I wasn't even sure I should go in. What was I gon do with some damn kids when I was one myself? Everything inside said leave them like their momma left me, but that wasn't me. Luka gripped my hand reassuring me that it was okay. Every emotion a person could have felt I went through but the two emotions that kept being at the forefront was envy because those so-called siblings knew a piece of our mother that I didn't. What was bad about me? What was I missing? And the second one was hurt because although Big Momma was there, she wasn't my momma and all my life I've felt unwanted, walking with a hole inside my heart feeling incomplete.

"Hello, my name is Nexus Grant, I'm here to see Doris Finnigan," I said as we slid her our Identification cards and walked through the metal detectors.

"She in the room down the hall to your left, 3rd door."

Knocking on the door, I walked in, and I was flabbergasted. Nyla and Nate were a splitting image of me when I was their age. Nate had a pessimistic look on his face while Nyla stared me down.

"Ms. Finnigan."

"Ms. Grant, thank you for coming today. Before you meet them, your mom left you a letter to read before you make a decision. So, if you follow me Mr…"

"Luka Musa."

"Musa, can go in the room with the kids," Ms. Finnigan suggested, and I followed her to the room next door holding the letter the hopefully answered some of the question that I wanted to know for years.

"Did you know her?"

"I did. She was my best friend for the last eight years."

"Did she talk about me? Why didn't you take the kids?"

"Not often because I think that was always a touchy subject for her, but I know she always kept tabs on you, and your grandma always wrote to her and sent pictures up until she died. Gawd, you look like her, I always thought Nyla was her twin, but I clearly was wrong."

"She wasn't the best she still was a…"

"Dead beat. Who she was for me and who was while knowing you is two different people. Why can't you take them?" I spoke through clenched teeth. Taking the woman in I could see she wasn't ugly. Dark skinned, short, hazel eyes with a nice shape. She looked all black and Finnigan is an Irish name.

"My husband and I have four kids, and we don't have the space for them." I nodded than proceeded to read the letter in my hand.

Nexus,

If you're reading this, I'm gone, and we never mended our relationship. I won't begin to apologize because I don't regret what I did. I was in love and hardheaded, and I ended up in an abusive relationship so, the first chance I got I ran. At that point in my life, I was selfish. I wanted to be grown and didn't know what that entailed. Eight months later, my mom called me and said your father dumped you on her and ask me to come back. It was you or me. I chose me. I am not saying this to hurt you, I want you to remember those words every time a man asks you to hinder your happiness. For your father, I gave everything and like the man he is, he took and took, and fucking took all the love, hope, and dreams that I had none to give you. Looking at you, being around you was a trigger, and I'm sorry for that. I kept telling myself that this was the right decision because how can you forgive me when I could not forgive myself? So, I found my second chance at happiness and then your siblings came along, and who knew I traded one monster into another. Your Big Momma always said I was looking for love in men that I couldn't find in my daddy and just maybe she was right. Nate and Nyla didn't ask to be here. I thought I had all the time in the world, seems like fate had to have the last laugh. I told them about you and what I thought you'd be like we celebrated your accomplishments and prayed for your bad days. I'm not here but you are, they got to know me, and you got to know Big Momma learn from each other and fix what I was too cowardly to do.

"Nate is a pretty boy and a ladies' man. He's full of laughs, but he sensitive when he gets to missing me. Let

him sleep with you and hold him. Nyla's a smart ass and if you're anything like sisters, you'll bump heads a lot but don't give up on them like I did you, have patience. I was at Big Momma's funeral I remember seeing you hold this chocolate drop hand as you cried in his neck. If you're anything like me, you're going to marry that man one day just make sure it's for the right reasons.

I left insurance in your name for you and your siblings. After you bury me, Nate and Nyla get fifty grand a piece and you get the rest. I love you no matter what your decision is.

Love,

Mommy

Tears spilled out my eyes. She had one thing right her ass was selfish. How could she expect me to do this? I pulled out my phone, she picked up on the first ring.

"What do I do, JuJu?"

"I can't answer that, but I will say this, for whatever reason you mom left you, but she missed out friend because you're the muthafuckin bomb. Do they look like her?"

"Nate does. He so handsome too. Now Nyla she a splitting image of me when I was that age. Part of me is curious and don't want to turn my back on them, and the other part of me saying just walk away and save the headache."

"Friend, who are you fooling? From the moment you knew of those kids you knew what you wanted to do. Don't be afraid. Embrace your future whatever it may be."

Juniece was right; I been made my decision. I wanted them to know me and vice versa. Looking through this glass. I saw Luka and the kids laughing. After saying a quick prayer, I walked in the room. I over to the kids and bent down in front of them.

"My name is Nexus Grant, and I'm your older sister, and if you want, I would love for you to come and live with me and my boyfriend."

"I'm Nate."

"Nyla. Momma told us about you, but you never visited."

"I didn't know about you until recently. I never met your mother but maybe you can tell me about her," I replied.

"I'd like that," Nate and Nyla said in unison.

"Okay, first I need you to fill out some paperwork and normally, we would have to investigation and clearances, but you sent off financials and backgrounds and everything checks out. Here are you cards that you will receive your stipend you'll get every last week of the month."

"Not that it's needed, so we will use it as

allowances."

"Okay then however you see fit. Their bags of things are with them and if you need anything don't hesitate to call. Be blessed Ms. Grant and Mr. Musa," she spoke before shaking our hand and leaving.

Thank God Luka's associate let us use their private plane because all I wanted to do was get home soon as possible. My classes started back Wednesday, and I still had to register the kids for school.

Nyla

"This is home, you can pick any room on the second level and unpack your things. I know everyone is tired so how about we order pizza and get to know one another" Nexus asked.

"I guess, but we only eat cheese."

"Me too. There are showers in each room and everything you need should be there as well. We will register y'all for school in the morning then go school shopping afterwards."

"Can we get a game system too?" Nate asked too giddy for my liking.

"Yea lil man, anything you want."

"We are not some charity cases that you can buy!" I yelled as loud as I could. My mom barely, mentioned her and when she did, it was about how she didn't even love her. I rather stayed in foster care then to beg my so-called sister for help.

"I'm not buying anyone." Nexus said in a matter-of-fact tone.

"Oh, so the new game system is what a sorry your mom died gift? You didn't even know her. hell, she never looked back to see if you were okay. Your just another wasted thing she left by the waist side," I managed to say as Nexus sent a slap to my face. Nexus hit me so hard, the paint on her wall chipped.

"Let's be clear I don't need you, ya grown little ass needs me. I spent most of my fucking life being not wanted and despite what your smart ass thinks, I didn't want you to feel like that. In my house, you will give me respect. You're lucky I showed up in the first place."

"Well, who the fuck asked you?"

"Listen here you little bitch, I chose you and Nate on my own accord."

"Stop fighting we're family," Nate cried. He was always sensitive and wore his heart on his sleeve. All he wanted was a real family. He always wanted to meet Nexus, and I was slowly ruining it for him.

"Hey, lil man go to your room and get your shower. I left some clothes on your bed I'll deal with this, I promise we gon be okay."

"Okay Luka."

"Baby girl take a walk and let me deal with this. Luka said in a low tone. She walked away with a defeated look on her face, and it made me feel a little bad. Luka demanded I sit down with the meanest mug on I ever saw. He was quiet but you could see the love he had for her. I was jealous. I wished I had someone fight for me the same way.

"You better not put your hands on me."

"Do you really think that's what we bought you here? Nyla, I don't know what you been through or what happiness looked like with your mother, but I do know that woman in there doesn't want to hurt you. Fix ya attitude and stop being a dick all your life because this isn't gon be to many chances of this bullshit."

Luka left me with my thoughts, leaving the room to pay for the pizza. I went to wash up for dinner and quietly sad down to eat.

"Where's Nexus?"

"She wasn't hungry she is sleeping. Tomorrow while I go to work, try not to make her angry too much. Eat as much as you want, there's juice and milk in the fridge, wipe down the table after you're done."

"Ny, you need to give her a chance."

"I know, Nate, but where was she when we needed her?" I started to cry, and Nate began to comfort me.

"She didn't know about us. Momma is gone and we're safe now, but you gotta stop blaming everyone for Momma's mistake," Nate whispered in my ear.

Nobody knew what we been through. When I heard of my sister, I knew that she was going to rescue us from that bitch we called a mother. When I dried my tears, I found a room and showered. As I washed my body, I cried again until the water ran cold, and I climbed in the bed, pulling the warm blankets over my head. She was five months too late. Just as I was about to close, I heard my door open and felt some lay behind me and wrap their arms around me. Her scent invaded my nostrils, and no words were said for quite a while.

"When I found out about having siblings, I was jealous. My whole life I've felt unwanted. I only saw her through pictures and my dad, lawd knows where he's at. After Big Momma died, it was just Lyric and me. It left me with a hole in my heart. I showed up because the moment I heard about you, I loved you and Nate. Nyla, I see hurt in your eyes if I did something tell me and I'll fix it."

"Where were you?"

"When? I'm right here" I rolled over, facing my sister for the first since we argued. She had tears clouding her vision while trying to wipe mine

"No. I needed you and you weren't there. I cried out for you, and you never came. She wasn't a good mother, and you didn't miss out on anything. That letter you read; Ms. Finnigan wrote. We needed you and you never showed, I ranted. She Grabbed my face, staring me in the eyes.

"What did she do? Tell me and I promise I will try and fix it."

My mouth became dry, and my hands began to sweat because of what I was about to reveal. Nate and I promised we wasn't going to say anything, but it was killing me, and I was steadily killing myself.

"You are safe now and whatever it is I promise we will get through this. Please Ny, what did she do?"

"On the outside, people thought we had it all and for a while we did too then she found out about her dying and started doing things. I caught her masturbating watching Nate shower, and I confronted her only to hear her laughing as if I told the funniest joke. She asked would I do anything to protect him? I answered without hesitation because Nate is everything good in the world and if she corrupted him, what would he become, you know? Little did I know the price I'd have to pay."

"What was the price?"

"Five months ago, a man came in my room and started touching me. I started crying asking begging for him only to look over and see the woman. I'll never forget her words."

"Do you not wish to protect your brother from little ole me? if you do, you will let Cole here fuck every fucking hole until he is satisfied."

"Why do this? Momma, please."

"See I tried to change. I thought I deserved happiness then suddenly that son of a bitch called God called for my life. I never had it easy this was my happiness or so I thought. So, I'm sorry my dear if I got to suffer you have too as well. I hope bitterness becomes you."

"My tears did nothing. So, I cried for you, and you never came."

"I didn't know but I promise you no one will ever hurt you again. Nyla, understand from this moment forward anyone who touches you I will see them dead myself."

"You promise?"

"Little sister, I promise this now and forever."

I cried. I cried again, and I cried until my voice

was horse, eyes bloodshot red, and my face was flushed red. That night my sister continued to hold me until I felt safe and for the first time since I been here, I felt her love for me. Now by no means was I cured or healed. In my mind, I was fucked up. I needed help and with it I was going to find the life that was fit to me.

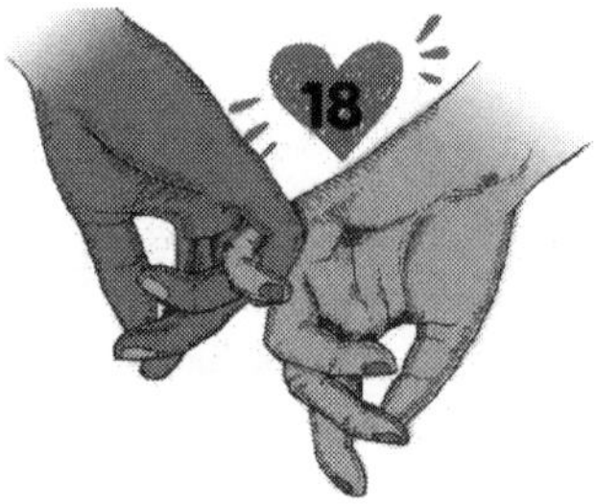

Julissa

The meeting

Everyone sat in the board room meeting in attendance. At the head sat Devin, then Kano, Luka Chance, JB, her sister, Marisol, and their daughter's Poetic, Sunny, Kennise, and Passion along with Lee, Brooke, and I to discuss the strip mall project.

"For the storefronts of the strip mall, which is in a prime location, have multiple offers and has agreed to pay thirty thousand monthly for the rent. As agreed, we discussed the women deciding what ten out of the twenty-nine stores and JB and family will have one of the major stores with rent free for two years for putting forty-nine percent of the money after that she will pay the rent required. The rest of the land is ours to do as we see fit."

"Ma what's the ETA on the construction of the mall?" Devin asked.

"The remodel will take a year and a half top if you want to cut corners which I don't recommend."

"I agree with Julissa, Devin."

"I understand. As for the store fronts let's do a bidding war for the remaining spaces."

"Yea but send out invitations to exclusive boutiques also."

"Will do, Kano, and with that we will take leave. Everyone," JB said as she and her family exited the board room. I was truly in awe at what we accomplished and it's all because he believed in us to have his back.

"Hey, Ma. Wassup with the status on the house?"

Chance asked Brooke.

"A hundred houses were built and auctioned off. All of them sold nicely and because of Lee's interior design on the model, she was hired for most of the projects. The apartments for low income are done and the waiting list is extensive. The transitional apartment for runaway teens are done as well and furnished with the basics. We are working with Ruth's House, as long as they complete the requirements, we're good to go."

"We're also placed a flyer for security guards. They won't be armed like the others, but they'll make decent wages to survive. Minor meetings will take place starting from this point until the girl's graduate. Only one of you guys have to attend. Emails will be sent out and everyone payments will be sent out as usual to their Swiss bank accounts."

"Everything sounds in order if we all agree, say I."

"I," everyone said in union.

"Meeting adjourned," I spoke. Once everyone was done, I picked up some Peaches Soul Food 'cause them ribs were the bomb. After I got my order, I called Juniece on my way home.

"Hey, Mommy what are you doing?"

"Picking up some Peaches Soul Food. What are you doing?"

"Waiting on your big head son-in-law to bring me some food now."

"I always knew he loved you. You waited so patiently, Juni. I'll admit his little ass damn near drove me up the wall, but you kept him in line. Juni, always be a man's peace never his problem and always encourage him to follow his dreams because he will always make sure to encourage yours."

"I will, Mommy. I got to go; he's walking through the door. Talk to you tomorrow." After saying my goodbyes, I pulled up and my lil sneaky link, Santino, was waiting at the door. All my life, I had been tied down for most of my twenties and early thirties and after that, I'd grieved my husband and as much as I loved him, our sex life was so boring that sticking a finger in my ass would have given me an orgasm and now, I wanted to enjoy sex without limits. My husband was traditional; it was always missionary, so I knew what sex was like. Next marriage, I didn't want to hide who I really was for a man to feel like a man. Santino was a lawyer who knew how to make time for what counts, and he proved time and time again that was me.

"Mi amore, your wine."

"Gracias, Papi. Cheers to good sexy and freaky encounters."

"Si l amour."

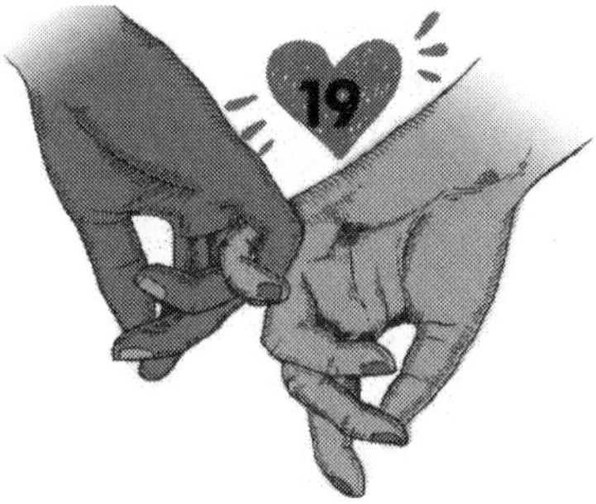

Demon

3 months later

I pulled her in for a hug. Her breasts being pushed against my chest had me ready to do all types of shit to her. I broke away from our hold and looked her up and down while licking my lips seductively, fighting the urge to devour her. I then lifted her chin and kissed her lips.

We began to kiss passionately for what seemed like eternity, but the softness of her plump lips wouldn't allow me to let go. When we finally pulled apart, giving each other room to breathe, she grabbed my hand and led me over to the bed.

We both were standing in front of the bed staring each other for a minute. She started unbuttoning my pants, then sliding them down while my dick went brick. After my pants and boxers were down, she pushed me, causing me to fall on my back. We were once again giving each other an intense stare. I watched her strip completely naked, so I took my shirt off and now I was naked as well. She then placed a soft kiss on my forehead, then went from there to my cheek then my lips. After placing a million kisses on my face, she ended up on my chest. Then from there, she made her way down to my hard dick. I was kind of over all the fore play shit and ready to dick her down.

My eyes were closed, enjoying the feeling of her warm mouth taking my dick whole. The way she was sucking, licking, and slurping had a nigga ready to cum. After she deep throated my shit one good time, I was shooting my seeds down her throat. Once I was done cumin, my dick was still standing. I ordered her to get on all fours before pushing her head down into the pillow. When she got in position, I rammed my dick in so hard causing her to wince in a pleasurable pain. While I moved in and out of her in a slow motion, I eased one hand to the front, so I could play with her clit while I penetrated her from the back.

The more I rubbed the wetter she got. I felt my nut rising, but I knew I wasn't ready to cum again. So, I pulled out for a little bit and slapped each ass cheek followed by me biting each one. The bites and the slaps must have been turning her all the way on because her ass was pleading for me to put the dick back in.

"Please put it back in… please," she whined, until I re-entered her.

"You ready for me to put it back in, huh?" I asked while slapping my dick on her ass before I slid it back in nice and slow.

Once I went back in, her shit was wetter than before. This time, I was ready to bring her to the ultimate climax. I was still using one hand to play with her clit while I stroked in and out of her. She started to tighten her pussy muscles on my dick, so I grabbed her hair and yanked her head back, so I can whisper in her ear.

"Stop doing that shit. I ain't ready to cum." I slapped her on her ass, smirking at the echo throughout the room.

"Why not, I want us to cum together?" she said in a seductive tone which drove me crazy. I continued to stroke her and flick my thumb across her clit while easing my other hand to her asshole. The sensation had her feeling so good that she started moving and moaning all crazy. The way her juices were gushing onto my dick, I knew I couldn't last much longer.

"Mmm... Hmm... girl throw that ass back, so we can buss this nut together." I hyped her ass up, and she did as she was told. A couple minutes later, we both were cumin right behind each other. She fell on the bed, and I fell right on top of her. We both laid there for a second until we processed what had just gone down.

"I think we need to use condoms because I think I am going get pregnant from Mr. Hanky." Juniece gushed.

"Shit, I already tasted the promise land and I'm not letting go of that feeling of my dick inside that juicy booty."

"Well, if I gain weight, getting knocked up by Mr. Hanky... "

"Then we just got a baby then. I have a meeting with the guys. Do you want me to pick up dinner or you going to cook?"

"I'm going to cook. Just hurry up and come back home. Thanksgiving is tomorrow, and I'm going to prepare my man a feast."

"I swear hearing that makes a nigga feel gooda then a muthafucka. What all are you cooking?"

"The ladies and I wanted to decide to keep trying infused foods. Nexus is doing the desserts; Lyric is doing themed drinks infused of course along with prep."

"Don't have that girl cooking fucking with our stomachs," I scolded. Shit, I loved Lyric and them Japanese dishes she created was on point, but her ass couldn't experiment on our asses on one of the important damn holidays out the year.

"I know better than that." Juicy laughed so hard looking at me, but she knew.

"What about our mothers and the kids?"

"So, I will be doing two of everything except for the meats. Those will have two types of sauces, one regular, the other infused. Can you pick up some items on your way home?"

"Yea, text the list to my phone. I'mma take a quick shower and head out."

"Okay, well I'm about to get some more rest before I have to get up and cook."

In no time, I was out the door and pulling up to Chance's house. Of course, they had us waiting outside because you could hear them going at it. Took them fool damn near an hour to open the door.

"My bad. Y'all know my baby jungle juice gets me in the mood," Chance joked, passing cups of jungle juice. He was right tho, that shit was hitting on everything.

"We outta beat yo ass. Shit, Nexus ass still bleeding walking around with that damn pamper on. Do they all wear them shits?" Luka asked.

"Yes," Chance and Demon said in unison.

"I don't know, I hope not."

"They asses like the Bratz dolls. They all in it together. Nexus walking around with that and a half - shirt on right now. The kids were clowning the shit outta her." We busted out laughing; that nigga Luka was a fool.

"How is it with the kids?"

"Man, Kano we are dealing with some shit, but we gon get through it tho. Nyla and Nate went through some sexual abuse and it's hard right now. In between that, we been packing like crazy to move to our estate next week. When are you guys moving?"

"We are moving next week too."

"I'm going to wait until after the new year and see if me and Drita baby got something. If she proves what I already know, I'mma ask her to move in with me."

"Shit I damn near moved everything except what on the first level. This is the last holiday, and I wanted each of you to know I appreciate each one of you my brothers for indulging in my childish whims. Take care of my wife until I come back, stick to the plan, and no matter what I love y'all, and I am coming back. Family over everything. salute."

"Salute."

We chilled for another hour joking and smoking. I was going to miss them, but when I finished the hardest part know, I was going begin my real journey with Juicy."

****

Thanksgiving Night

After saying goodbye to the last bit of guests, I went to search for Juicy so we could finish cleaning up the kitchen and get a lil night cap in. Instead, I found her bent over the toilet in our hallway. Rushing over, I held her hair as she threw up her intestines.

"You sure Lyric didn't cook?" I joked.

"I'm sure. Maybe I'm just exhausted I did a lot today and this was my body saying to relax."

"Maybe you're right. I'll run you some bath water and you can relax." I left before waiting for her reply. I ran a nice bubble bath and added some Calgon and baby oil inside. Since Jesscenda and I broke up and Ma had already moved into her new house, we had been staying there so it wasn't no confusion.

"Baby girl, come on, I'll clean the kitchen."

"Okay, baby."

It took no time to clean the kitchen and wipe down everything. I bagged all the trash in the house and took it outside. Soon as I lifted the top, gunshots ranged out, and as soon as the shock wore off, my heart began to ache because I was leaving baby girl. It was easy to say I could do it, but it was a whole another thing to do it. I was dying, and I never said.

.

"Baby everything……...NOOOOOOOOOOOOOOOOO! baby don't leave me. Pleaseeeeee, you said forever. SOMEONE HELPPPPPP!!!!"

"Ju…Ju…. Juicy booty, I love you," I whispered before everything went black.

Juniece

I laid in my bed with tears falling out my eyes while holding a positive pregnancy test. I couldn't believe this; my world was gone just as it was beginning and hurt from losing Devin finally broke me. Everything smelled like him and everywhere in this apartment reminded me of him. Going to college seemed impossible because I barely left the house, let alone washed my ass. My momma had to take off work just to make sure I was okay. When I heard the news, all the color left my face. My breath was gone, and my eyes became dull as if life was no longer in them. It was like I died that I tried to kill myself. There was no life without Devin so how did they expect me to survive? In my mind I was brain dead. I had cut my phone off and told everyone to let me be in peace. None of them listened. Most days. the girls rotated giving me sponge baths and making sure I ate, and the men would always take turns running around and doing chores and walking the dogs. I received a letter from Devin's attorney about his estate, and I had yet to open it. Money didn't move me. he did and he knew it. I wanted so badly to cuss his ass out for leaving me. I wanted to abort this baby cause how was I going to do it all alone? But then it was all I had left of him. I was a lot of emotion, and nothing was clear.

"Juniece, are you ready yet?" my mother asked, walking in the room with an all-black dress that looked painted on, and some Gucci pumps Demon brought her for her birthday and opening the blinds in my room.

“No, Mom, I’m not going I can’t do it all those tramps going to be there and what am I supposed to do?” I cried.

“You can and you will because I raised you. Devin died and it’s fucked up he left you alone. Right now, nothing makes sense. Those tramps didn’t mean shit, but you did. So, what you’re going to do is get up and wash your ass because right now this room smell just like a can of throw that ass. And wash your hair and get dress to say goodbye. You will do it with class and then figure out what life looks like without him because the world doesn’t stop when death happens. You’re pregnant and he’s not here but you have a village,” my mother, Julissa, ranted over and over again. Within thirty minutes, I was dressed in an all-black pants suit with a black veil with light makeup.

****

William Murphy’s *Praise is what I do* trumpeted throughout the church as we made our way to the front. I couldn’t come to terms with the fact that Demon was gone. I didn’t want to accept it. Our last conversation was an argument and knowing that I would never have the opportunity to apologize was killing me. He didn’t know of what we created and that hurt more than anything.

I took slow, long strides to the front hoping that someone would tell me that I was being pranked but this was my reality. He wasn't coming back.

It was my turn to view him, and I felt the pits of my stomach attempting to erupt. I felt my soul doing somersaults in my chest while my chest heaved up and down. Anxiety crept its way in, causing me to gasp for air as I stared at him. He was at peace, but he was bringing me so much pain. Devin had no idea how much his death had taken its toll on me. He had no idea how much I truly cared about him, and he never would. Say I love you wasn't enough. I rubbed my hand down his handsome face and the song I had on repeat came out.

"I think about the years I spent just passin' through

I'd like to have the time I lost and give it back to you

But you just smile and take my hand

You've been there, you understand

"You promised me, you wouldn't leave. You left, what do I do now. You lied to me, Devin, you are fucking liar. Why didn't you take me with you? You promised," I cried as the tears cascaded down my face, banging on the casket until my mother walked up in tried to pull me away.

"Juni baby let's go sit down."

"No mom 'cause he is playing, baby get up and show them you're playing so we can go home. Devin get up and let's go home."

"Sis he's gone" Drita said just above a whisper. Turning round I fell into Drita's arms and cried so loud that you could hear down the block and around the corner. It was like life was playing a sick joke, but I was waiting to laugh because I was completely breaking.

"D, he promised me he wouldn't leave, and he left, sis."

"It's going to be okay . . . ."

"Oh lawd, oh lawd it's true!" I heard from behind me, causing me to turn around.

My nostrils flared while my lips twisted, seeing Kano's mom making her way towards me. Her eyes were bucked letting me know that she was high as hell as she stepped closer.

"Lawd! Take us all, Father! Take us all and spare none of us." She grabbed the casket and rocked back and forth. "Devin, wake yo' ass up!" She started rocking him, and I grabbed her.

"Shelly Ann, sit yo' ass down and let that boy rest," Luka's mom, Lee, demanded, grabbing her opposite arm, and pulling her away.

Shelly Ann snatched away and snarled at Lee. "OH, go to hell Lee with your fat ass. You always think you better than—"

Kano rushed over and grabbed his mother aggressively while looking into her eyes.

"Yo, you serious right now? Why the fuck would

you come in here like that?" he fumed, holding her by elbow. She twisted and turned to break free but that only made his grip tighten.

Guests continued walking down the aisle unbothered by her actions until she stopped and picked up one of the flowers, launching it at Lee. Missing her by an inch, the flower landed on Brook's foot, causing Brook to grill her.

"See now you done fucked up." Brook rushed over and grabbed Shelly Ann by her nappy hair, and they started to tussle.

It was more than embarrassing that those two grown women were acting that they, but it was to be expected coming from Shelly Ann. She didn't know how to sit back and relax because she was never sober enough.

As they carried Shelly Ann out, she used her feet against the wall to try and stay inside, but Kano wasn't having it.

"Let me go so I can beat her ass. You got it coming, bitch." Brook passed Lee her bag and started wrapping her dry ponytail around until it was in a ball.

"I got the bike, Holiday!" Chance ran back and forth waving Brook's wig in the air. Snatching it from him, Brook placed it back on her head and adjusted her skirt.

"That's a damn shame y'all acting like this at this boy's funeral and—"

"You shut your ass up, Pam. Always thinking you better than somebody. Her crackhead ass started with me and Brooke first!" Lee spat.

Pam was Devin's aunt, and she didn't play when it came to her nephew. She loved Devin like he was her own son, so I knew that her pain was on a different level.

"Everybody get out!" Pam erupted with her veins protruding out of her forehead. Everybody looked on as she proceeded to walk towards the crowd, making them turn around.

"Y'all have lost your damn minds coming in here disrespecting my nephew like this," she continued her rant.

"We loved him t"

"Like hell y'all did!" she hissed back at Brook. "And you the main one. Coming up in here fighting like y'all still in high school. You let a crackhead get the best of you and—"

"That's still my fucking mama!" Kano roared making his way back in. "Y'all not gone keep talking shit about her like a nigga ain't standing right here. We all fucked with Devin, so you can miss me with that get out shit. We have—"

Pam's head cocked to the side, causing Kano to halt with his statement and size her up. Devin's funeral had turned into a nightmare, and it was all because grown ass women didn't know how to conduct themselves. It baffled me how everyone portrayed to love and miss him, yet they were ruining our final goodbye. Pam kept acting like Kano wasn't her nephew too. We knew how much she loved Devin and hated Kano and no matter how everyone told her that wasn't right, Pam just flat out didn't care.

"Kano." She chortled. "You got some nerve waltzing your ass back in here defending that animal you call a mother. Look at what she did!" She pointed at the damaged flowers and broken vase. "She came in here and acted an ass because she was high out of her damn mind. I have every right to put everyone out. My sister just lost her son behind your shit. I just know it. Devin was a good boy. I don't need this extra stress, look at me. Then, got little fat shawebbie crying like her hoe ass really loved him."

All eyes darted towards the front pew as I sat with Drita with my head down, sulking. Not once did anyone acknowledge how I felt because they were too busy acting like they were circus clowns. A family had just taken an extreme loss and here we were making a mockery of it. Honestly, I was too tired to say anything but that didn't stop my momma getting up to her face.

"Bitch. you had done really violated now. First no one disrespects my child like that. Pam. since you walked in you been on bullshit with your tacky ass perpetrating. I raised Devin when no one else would and through every accomplishment I never saw you. Always too busy to show up because let's face it a man was more important and dogging Kano out when he has been the only consistent family in his life. All that mouth but please remember how you took my eight thousand dollars without so much as a second thought to stay away, with your sorry ass!" my momma shouted, shocking the whole congregation.

Kano licked his lips and ran his hand over his head before looking back towards the church doors to make sure Shelly Ann wouldn't come back in.

"Pam with all due respect, I came to show love to my cousin, my brother, and regardless of what Dukes did that ain't got shit to do with all these people. Everybody loved Devin. It's just sometimes our actions get the best of us. Don't hold that against her when your dirty laundry was just aired out."

My eyes widened shocked that Kano didn't go off. Even though Shelly Ann had been battling her addiction for a long time. he didn't let that stop his love for her. He didn't see her the way we all did, but he didn't ignore it neither.

Shaking her head, Pam broke down and rushed off towards her sister. Sitting beside her, they consoled one another while we stood on confused.

"This some bullshit!" Luka fussed, running his hand down his face. "Nigga been gone ten minutes and shit already falling apart." He shook his head while everyone began to take their seats.

The funeral lasted about an hour, and I was pretty much over it. It didn't matter how many people had come out; I didn't feel that no one besides his family's pain was equivalent to mine. I broke down as I watched them close the casket and carry it out. Demon was gone, and there was nothing I could do about it.

Four months later

"Ahhhhhhh, get this baby out now!" I screamed out loud 'til my voice became loud. Ya girl was blossoming. After that whole Demon fiasco, I got myself together. I realized my cousin, Sia, was right. I should have left Demon alone and gave Duke a real chance and every day, he was proving to be the right decision. He even invested in my business. I opened up Stylz by Cenda which was my hair salon with connected boutique. I needed growth and although I was still growing, I needed to let go. It took me a long time to realize different is okay. Now Fat A ss and I will never be okay but letting a man go for a man I actually cared about felt right. I'd been doing therapy and I wanted to know what my idea of love looks like. Duke and I moved to a four -bedroom, three -bath out Delaware, and I really loved the atmosphere. We made time for each other, we had date night, we traveled. I just hoped when the baby came nothing changed.

"Baby girl, you can do it. Push that shit out. You can do it."

"Duke, fuck you and that 'look who got a surprise' ass dick."

"Pushhhhh, Jesscenda you can do it!" the doctor screamed.

"She out," the doctor announced and laid this beautiful, little girl on my chest. Skin -to- skin -skin, and I didn't feel any connection. She looked like me and yet she resembled both men.

"Excuse me, Doc. How long before we can do a DNA test?"

"A simple swab, and we will rush the results," the doctor replied before walking out.

"You couldn't wait a day."

"Nah, I want to know she's mine before I fall in love raising that nigga seed and shit. I love the shit outta you and in all reality, you the one who gon' carry my last name, but in the reality she's not mine you willing to give her up for a future with me?" I looked at this man to see if he was really serious, and I'll be got damn he was. Now I know y'all saying, *bitch. you gotta be stupid,* but y'all didn't understand this beautiful child I birth didn't feel like mine, and this man loved me when I didn't love myself. He took me at my worst and built me up when Demon walk away from me without so much as a goodbye. This choice was hard and simple at the same time.

"Duke, I don't know. I love you, but I need time to think about it." Could I honestly give away a child I carried for nine months? Would I cry if she wasn't Duke's, and if I she wasn't would he allow me to see her? All these questions weighed me down. That's why I couldn't believe in God, he never gave me anything. Women like me ain't wrong for stealing happiness and breaking up homes because nine times outta ten we never had the option to genuinely have it, so we stole it as if it was a high price piece of jewelry.

"Cool, I'll be back in a little bit," Duke announced before walking out the door before I could even reply.

I stared down at the engagement ring Duke placed on my hand a month ago and wondered why love was so hard for me. I thought with Demon gone, all the puzzles to my life would fall into place, sadly that I what I get for assuming. Tears fell as I silently cried myself to sleep.

What you did
Yeah, you know I love you, but I can't forgive it
You could tell me stay but I have to go

-

Mahalia

Juniece

Eight years later

"Ma'am your total is 431.92," the young cashier spoke in an upbeat tone.

Today was Friday, and I had to reup on everything. Shit thank God we had the dogfood delivered every month. I took out my debit card and paid for all my items.

"Here you go. Keep the change."

"Thank you." The cashier happily nodded.

"Ms. s. Juniece you need help today?"

"Sure, Kalen." Kalen lived in our houses we put up for sale. His mom, Angel, worked at our leasing office and his dad and older brother worked as security guards.

Kalen was a straight A student, and he worked on weekends at the family grocery store that the whole family owned. When he was done, I closed my trunk and handed him a twenty as a tip before getting in my car and pulling up. I had been up since six a.m. paying bills and going over contracts. I also took out some lamb chops out of the fridge that I marinated in water, orange peelings, and apple cider vinegar. When I unwrapped it, washed it and placed them in a baking dish and seasoned it with lemon and garlic, pepper, Sazon, and rosemary and placed them on the grill, pairing it with corn on the cob and yellow rice. When I was done, I washed the kid's' laundry and worked on payroll which was damn near a three-hour job. Thank goodness we had a security team who picked and dropped the kids off at school because we had enough stuff on our plates. On school days, I always made sure cook early so my kids didn't eat too late. My phone rung as I was placing our dinner In Tupperware containers.

"Hey, Momma."

"Hey, Juni, where my grandbabies at?"

"They on their way home. What are you doing?"

"I'm about to have a late lunch with Lee and Brook, and I was wondering do you need me to do anything before our family trip for Davina's birthday?"

"Oh yeah can you make a cake?"

"For my grandbabies, I will make two. I can't leave my other baby out."

"Okay, how are you?"

"I'm happy baby girl. What about you? Any new men, lately?"

"Ma you know me work and my kids are all I know. I still have the shirt he slept in the night before, and I sleep with it to remember his smell and I, I still have glimpses of how he touched me and reminisce of the all the conversations we use to have. Replacing that is impossible because he's gone and never is coming back, Mom. So, I pour double the love into our kids, so they never feel like they're missing out on nothing,"

"Oh, Juniece I wish I could have shield you from this hurt but death in inevitable. I remember you once asked me if dad would walk through the door what would you do? Would you scream where you been? Or would you accept the second chance given?" I laughed a little bit because I remember that.

"And you said you would hold him and never let him go."

"That's right because no matter the issues he was a good man and boy, did he love us. Now I ask you those same questions."

"Without a doubt take the second chance given because my heart won't let him go. Maybe I'm crazy, or dumb as hell, but Momma nobody in this world can love me like him. The kids coming in I'll call you later and please stop letting them drive the golf carts."

"Okay Juni, talk soon baby girl." She rushed me off the phone. My momma stayed spoiling my kids and that was the issue. Even though we lived in a gated community. we all still lived a fair distance, so we drove our golf carts and my momma let my kids get away with murder.

"Hey, babies how was school?"

"Good! Momma, am I going to see Jezebel today?"

"Devina, don't call her that and no not if you don't want to. Why do you ask because you haven't been over there in years?"

"She had Dana text me. I just wanted to stay with you and sissy and help out at the studio. She not even consistent and every time I go over there, her husband looks at me with disgust and them kids run around like their head chopped off." Devina ranted.

"Okay, baby girl but were not going to be there long today. Ja'sai, how was school dinky?"

"Good, Mommy. Can we go home and watch Daddy again?" my youngest asked.

Here I was twenty-seven with two kids. Soon as Devina was born and Duke found out she wasn't his, he made Hoe Ass choose and of course, she dropped the baby off here. Not that I mind. From the moment I saw her I knew she was meant to be mine. She couldn't stand going over Jesscenda's house because they always treated her like she didn't belong. Shit, it was quite a few occasions when I had to go over there and yank that hoe up for whopping my baby when she didn't whoop them bad ass kids she was raising. Ja'sai and Devina were three months apart, but you couldn't tell them nothing. When Devin died, I found myself lost and if it wasn't for Stupid Ass dropping off my bonus baby, I don't know where I'd be. To protect myself, I had her sign over her rights so she couldn't take my baby back when she didn't even deserve her.

What mom gives their child up for a man anyway? After r a few weeks, I re-enrolled in college and then a month later, Ja'sai entered the world, and I realized the hardest parts of being a parent was having two babies at the same time, but everyone helped. They were my village. And everyone lived on the land we own so that was a blessing in disguise. The papers the lawyer left from Devin were all of his accounts and me and my girls having a seat on the board of Phantasia after we all graduated with at least one degree. Proud to say, I graduated with a business degree and a communications degree. I'll let the girls tell you about theirs. Once we found out the girls did their research and came up with a dope idea involving cannabis, we instantly invested in their dream. We took three stores and combined them and named it Elevation which was a weed dispensary on one side, another level was a soul food restaurant with infused cannabis, the last level of the store was a hookah lounge that always had a line always wrapped around the corner and a three-year waiting list to host parties because we had a nice big dance floor.

I also had a mix fit work out studio that I owned called Roadz. I was still a big girl, but I wanted to be healthy with a body, and I encouraged women to do that too. We had our own line of alkaline water and smoothie bar inside with a sauna and exclusive yoni line because who don't love their yoni?

Raising my girls without that man truly hurt me to the core, so I made all the videos I had of us. into a movie. Me and kids would always watch and play new video games and eat candy like Devin and I. and I was still bad. That man gave me the gift of never having to struggle and always being able to provide for our kids. When he died, we were staying in our new house all the rooms were empty for me to decorate except for the game room and his man's den. We loved anime we always said when we had kids that we'd travel there as a family. so over the years we added the animes we loved to the game room; it had every game system ever created.

"That's fine. I can get a matcha green tea smoothie," Devina declared.

"Ooh me too, Momma."

"Fine, greedy butts. Go get your coats. While I talk to your Uncle Kano."

"Hello."

"Hey sis, what yo big headed ass doing?"

"I'm about to head to Roadz for to get some paperwork about the winery."

"How is it looking?"

"Good for the most part if Chance can work with the numbers for the inn, I think this could be profitable."

"I ran the numbers, and we are actually under budget. Luka will finish the paperwork once everything is done. You are dropping the girls off later?"

"Not tonight. Where's Drita?"

"Downstairs fighting with your niece about doing her hair, and she told me to tell you to let your kids know not this year with them damn dogs," Kano joked.

One thing Drita hated was doing KK hair because her little ass was so tender headed and refused to stay still. We had six dogs. Natsu, Lucy, Grey, Juvia, Gajeel, and levy. They were all Italian Cane Corso with red eyes that made their coats shine even more. That I signed us up to take dog training courses to make sure my kids didn't get hurt 'cause I didn't play about that shit. So anytime we carried a litter, the girls trained them, named them from an anime they watched, and gave them out to the family as gifts, but Drita always claimed we give her the retarded dogs because they keep stressing her out. To be fair tho Luffy and Zoro were twins and only listened KK bad ass.

"Well tell her I'll call her tomorrow. The girls want to want to do movie night, but I'll talk to you, soon."

"Girls, come on."

"Ma, why don't you throw that ass back?"

"Ja'sai your betta watch that mouth. Where did you hear that from anyway?"

"At Auntie Drita's house, she was telling Auntie Lyric that it's been so long since you threw that ass back that it's probably cobwebs on that coochie."

"What I tell you about staying out of grown folks' business?"

They asses get on my nerves. for years the girls been trying to get me to date, and I'll admit I'd tried, but they never quite felt right. I had the latest cars and a beautiful house, but if I could do anything it would be to have my first love back. My mind said it was time, yet my heart said wait.

"That I need to stop being nosey and focus on the business that pays me."

"Told you," Devina taunted.

"Shut it, Vina."

"Listen I only loved one man in my life and that man was your dad and he was my best friend. That type of love is hard to find. So, when and if I meet someone as great as your dad comes along, we will discuss it."

"Okay."" they whined in unison.

When we got out, the girls and I went our separate ways. We also had a kid's gym as well, and they loved them smoothies I'd created from popular animes and fairytales. When I got to my office, I went over every email and read over the employee evaluations. I poured myself in my work. I was lonely and even eight years later, I couldn't allow a man to claim what was his. What was supposed to turn into picking up papers turned into a six-hour shift because one of our instructors called out that was supposed to teach three different classes. When I pulled up Drita, Lyric, and Nexus was calling me back-to-back while I was standing in the driveway. Suddenly, I felt like shit was going to hit the fan.

Demon

Eight years ago

"Welcome back to the land of the living. The first three targets are all disclosed in this folder between missions. Your handler will be Styx. Only my family will deliver the targets; anything other than that Styx will be who you will call. Also, during your mission, we promise to update you with pictures and videos involving your family and any business as promised." JB stated.

I missed Juicy like crazy, but I was doing this for us. Shit. living to go back home was signing my own death warrant, and I didn't want to cause Juicy harm. I did enough shit already. I watched how she cried over my casket and how my family reacted, and it tore me up. Kano, Chance, and Luka knew the truth and were only to contact me if it was important. But what fucked me up when I found out Juniece was pregnant with my seed, and I wouldn't be there for none of that shit, and the guilt was slowly eating away at me.

"Hey, handsome. I'm Styx, I'll be here to handle all your needs," she openly flirted. Styx was far from ugly, lil momma was sexy as fuck. She just wasn't my baby. Styx was 5-foot-6, brownskin complexion, beautiful hazel sepia shaped eyes, with a fat ass, and perky as titties enough to fill a nigga's mouth. Even the sundress clung to her body like she had purpose.

"Demon, focus you got a goal. First hit is in Dubai, your plane takes off in fifteen. Styx, you're here for support. Anything other than that is not for you, stay in your lane. That man has a family he's going back to, and you're going to be left scorned with a wet ass. Don't be messy," JB warned. Soon as we boarded the plane, Styx went in, she was on a mission. She wanted me and was willing to do anything to prove it.

"So, why do they call you Demon?" Styx flirted as she opened her legs, giving me a peak at her pretty pink pussy before crossing her legs. I looked; I was a man but lil mama was going to have to do more than thot shit to get this python I carried around.

"Nah the mothers from my neighborhood use to call me that shit because I was always up to no damn good."

"And are you no damn good?"

"I mean it depends on who's asking," I responded, firing up the weed and luring her into my trap.

"What if I'm asking?"

"You'd still be asking. Styx I'm not going to downplay your sexiness, but you are too damn thirsty. Why do they call you Styx?"

"You ever seen the movie Sparkle? It was my momma's favorite and the main characters' love story just stuck with her hence the name Sparkle Styx Dixon. So, you got a lil girl, huh? You are faithful or do you like to have fun."

"Let's get some shit straight really quick. One, I don't have a little shit. My wife is big. Bodacious, gorgeous, ass woman, and she is none of your concern. Lusting after dick without knowing a nigga more than a half of an hour."

"I wasn't…."

"You were and because you look the way you do, you thought it was okay. "Styx had that video vixen look that niggas dreamed about; I just wasn't one of those men. For the most part, my relationship with Styx was cool as years passed, and I remained loyal that I wasn't until Tahiti six years later we actually slept together and before y'all scream y'all disappointed in ya boy remember I am a nigga. Watching my wife live life without me killed me slowly and it wasn't nobody's fault. I'm no dummy; I told Styx just enough. I never disclosed anything about Juicy and my kids but that never stopped her from telling me how she had a boyfriend who was extremely clingy, and family who financially dependent on her. It started off fun, no attachments but then she started asking to stay all night and make me food and dates. Styx saw me as her savior and in another time, I very well could have been just that. She wanted me, and I didn't want her like that.

STYX

That man before me had to be specially crafted I wanted him something bad and I was going to have him. Now before you haters get to hating and being dick riders let me introduce myself. The name is Styx, just like Cher or Madonna, I was a star in the making. I wasn't ugly either most people said I resembled Zoey from *Grown-ish* just a little thicker, so trust I never had man that I couldn't have, yet this nigga did, and he checked my ass which had my pussy dripping from the smoothness of his voice. Right now, he didn't want me because of his bitch left behind but give it time, I was gonna fuck his life up with this tight ass cat. After excusing myself, I went into the cock pit and got Mickey to come into the restroom.

"Oh, you want this dick after you was flirting in my face damn near begging that nigga for his dick, and I know you're about to say I ain't ya nigga and that's fine until I'm entertaining the next bitch and here you go wanting to lay claim. And I know D, and he isn't the problem, you are," Mickey whispered through clenched teeth.

Mickey wasn't your average ass dude. He had been a pilot for over nine years, and we met on my first mission in Jamaica. He resembled Morris Chestnut, had his own, and spoiled me rotten and wanted to give me all the things I craved yet something inside me thought I would lead this man to ruin.

"Can we just fuck without arguing for once?"

"We could but we are not you gon' do what you want and every time your desperate ass gets disappointed, you come running to me and like a sick puppy, I am waiting because despite what you think, I love your slow ass but no more. In the words of T.I when you see me in the streets remember you don't know me. when you want to slide down this fat ten-inch snake remember you don't know me and when whine for this tongue action, bitch remember you don't know me." Mickey complained, walking out with the look of disgust on his face. Not even letting me get a word. I wanted Mickey but Demon, I wanted him more. Pulling out my rose toy, I pleasured myself, pulling on my pretty B-cup titties 'til I came all over my fingers and licked myself dry.

****

Present Day

Devin

"I see the target. She in the room with two men."

"Eliminate them all and get out of there. After today, you are a free man. The airplane is up in twenty minutes," JB responded.

Looking into the scope of my M82 sniper rifle and just as smooth as butter can spread. the niggas in that office dropped one by one. Grabbing my gun, I ran down the stairs and hopped in the car on the way to the hangar. This shit was surreal, I was finally going home.

"Excuse me, beautiful, can I get a Crown straight I asked after stopping the attendant and leaned my head back in the chair thinking of the many outcomes that awaited me. Hopefully, I had a family to go home to.

"So that's it. No more late nights and early mornings. You going to let us be done?"

"Styx don't start this shit. We fuck six times total. You didn't stay in my bed overnight, didn't go on any dates, we all knew what it was from the beginning."

"I love you Styx pleaded.

"Well see that's your problem because the feelings not mutual. Your ass was so thirsty that you waited six years to taste my dick only to turn around and lay claim to something that was never you're in the first place. I wish you the very best, but you have nothing over this way."

"I'll tell her about us," Styx threatened.

She was dumb as fuck. She thought her pussy would sway how I felt about her. Even after all the years, I still remember how wet Juicy was when we made love the first time and the sweetness of her pussy flowed on my tongue. It was more than that though, and Styx could never compare. Shit, I wished I never gave Jesscenda the time I did and going forward, I was going to show Juniece everyday how appreciative I am that she chose to love me.

"Sir we are arriving at your destination as we speak."

"Thanks, lil mamma."

"That's it?"

"The woman I chose means more to me than time itself. She makes me better. Without her, I can't be me. So, yea, that's it and that's all." Without so much as a goodbye, I walked off that plane to never look back. I was home, and the smell of the D.C air smacked in the face. Shit, I wandered if them fools would even remember me. Back then I was boney, strong lil nigga. Now you couldn't say shit. I swole up eating all of them foreign foods and worked out a lot. The dreads that once flew down my back was now long and curly. With some gold tips in my mouth that paired well will my brownish, goldish eyes. Soon as hit the bottom of the plane stairs my niggas, my brothers were standing next to a beautiful ass 2022 money green Aston Martin. It was my favorite color.

"Welcome home, nigga Kano expressed, pulling me in a hug over the years we talked but it was nothing like seeing the family in the flesh.

"Thanks, cuz, you handle that shit I asked you to do?"

"Do you even have to ask?" he replied, smiling like a Cheshire cat.

"Cutie ya ass grown up now but who lil mama on the plane staring you down like you stole her pocketbook?" Luka asked, pulling me in for a hug.

"That was Styx . She was my back up."

"This nigga here. You fucked shawty didn't you? Sis gon' kill us all. She been going to the gun range since her freshman year of college and got these twin 9 mm Glocks. Her shit better than yours." Chance dumb ass spoke like he was terrified of my harmless Juicy booty.

Styx

Now I wasn't crazy or naïve. I was a big girl, and I knew what it was from the start, and I knew what I was doing when I tried to make something out of nothing, I watched him from the plane, and I had thoughts to go break up this man's relationship and for what? To look like the crazy bitch in every book. This wasn't my story and despite whatever feelings I had for Demon, I didn't know him because he never allowed me to. I couldn't even tell you his birthday because he only celebrated his wife's birthday. Taking one final look because this truly was goodbye I waved. Mickey was true to his word and cut me off. I heard he was dating a chick he met from Egypt, and she was really feeling him. My story gon' come and be my story to fight for my man because I didn't appreciate him when I had him. I took him for granted and I was slowly learning my lesson. He switched planes, so I no longer saw him on missions. When I was with Demon, sex was great, but when I'm with Mickey it was earth shattering. I had this idea of what I wanted in a man; I thought I needed a thug like Demon, but shit mice could be dangerous too. Since Mickey blocked my number, I had to use my work phone to text him.

10:15 AM (7 minutes ago)

ME:

I made a lot of mistakes with us you were fighting for me, and I took you for granted. It's been 5 years, and I miss you like crazy. I was running away from here because I thought I would destroy you, but baby don't get it fucked up, Mama's coming home to claim her man. Tell the bitch she got to go.

Future: *What the fuck man. It wouldn't work out with you and Dee huh, and now you want me. I ain't playing second field to no nigga, and I got a bitch to do all the shit you did. Stop thinking that somebody waiting around for your ass. Despite what you think, I loved your selfish ass; hell, I still do but I can do bad on my own.*

ME: *Mickey, you got that. I'll let it rocks now, but I'm coming home, and you already know how I roll.*

Future: *Fuck off my line you don't deserve this dick and you, damn sure don't deserve me desperate ass bitch.*

Me: 🥺🥺🥺 *That is how you giving it up? I get it I deserve it I was desperate for something that never belonged to me, but you Mickey Shaft Night. Your heart belongs to me, and I'm claiming every mother fucking part. See you soon, bae.*

I cut off my phone, getting ready for take-off. A tear slid down my face ass I asked myself what I was thinking I was so damn selfish and stupid. Wait for my novella *"Lil Mama- Craved- A-Savage."*

Drita

"Bae, you didn't hear me calling your ass," Kano bassed raising his voice to get my attention Wearing his dreads in two braided cornrows, shirtless, and some basketball short and slides on looking like the ultimate fuck nigga. A bitch was still obsessed like the day he walked in Red Lobster.

"No, Kano I answered, irritated. Kiandra be still, your dad isn't going nowhere you got two braids left."

"But Mommy, it hurts." KK cried.

As Luffy and Zero started barking like they did anytime she got her hair done. I was on my last braid then added beads. One thing I didn't play about was my daughter looking more than her age, and I didn't care how busy I have been. I made time for my husband and my kids.

"Ms. Drita is KK ready to leave for her playdate?" our house cleaner, Leah, asked. Now before y'all be in my business about me having a maid know that I wanted my child to have the best. She wasn't raising my child, but Leah cooked, cleaned, and tutored KK. She was learning Spanish, Japanese, Bulgarian, and some broken English's so she was a keeper.

"She's ready. I packed her bag as well."

"Okay, see you later pudding pop," I cooed to my daughter.

KK was the very definition of my love in human form. She embodied everyone of Kano's promises to me, and I was truly happy. After the cabin, Kano kept his word. We started dating and getting to know each other, and I started working for him. I started college and realized as hard as it was it felt good to do something truly for myself. I graduated with a business degree and culinary arts. I also opened a kids clothing store called Pretty Styles, which was doing pretty well for itself. When I graduated, Kano gave me the gift of security. For a whole day, I cried because no man ever gave me this and although he didn't know me, he still saved me. My mom found out where I lived from my cousin, and when I refused to let her in my space, she broke into my apartment and sold my shit. It hurt so bad that she couldn't understand what that did to me.

Of course, soon ass Kano found out he made me move in with him temporarily, I suggested but coming home to him, cooking dinner, listening to rap songs, and doing tik toks made me hesitant to leave. I stayed though and let that man fill me up with all the love I could take. Two year later, I gave birth to Kiandra, and I can truly say that I was in love with this man. Now I'm two months pregnant with my son, Klaus Danger Coles. "Bye, baby girl."

"Bye Mommy and Daddy."!" she shouted, running out the door for her play date.

"You still going to work, tonight?"

"Yea, the girls, and I are doing the poetry slam, Why Wassup, Puddin'?" I asked as I wrapped my arms around Kano's neck, planting kisses on his big full lips.

"The guys were thinking we'd step out tonight. It's been crazy busy lately, and I want to take my fiancée' show how much I appreciate her," Kano said between the kisses, sliding his tongue in my mouth as I sucked on his tongue gripped my ass.

"It has been so long, daddy, but I don't want Juniece feeling like the fifth wheel in a group for couples. That seems insensitive babe, don't you think?"

"Don't worry about, sis I got a surprise for her and plus, you don't even need to be around all that smoke anyway."

"I'm not, we going to be in a VIP having mocktails, and Juniece going read a poem that it and that's all. Have a little bit of food and relax. Then come and let my man fuck me silly and if he gives me that proper dick, I might let him knock that pussy up again after I drop his son off," I cooed.

Now ladies like I said before that man does all for me without asking, he is a great father and is available for us because we matter to him. Not once has a bitch stepped to me about my man, he is home before eleven unless he is hanging with the boys, so my pregnancy was stress free. Having this man's kids was not a problem when daddy displayed big dick energy. Well, shit it was already four, and we had to there a 7:30. I'd might as well love on my man.

"Shittt you ain't saying nothing but a word then 'cause daddy always giving you proper dick that's why you pregnant now for doing it on the pastor's car during church." We both laughed.

"Come on daddy let me bathe you clean," I seductively whispered, kissing Kano's lips while peeling off my clothes and walking to our shower.

"Damn Kano moaned salivating at the mouth. I turned the water on to get hot. I placed my hair up naked as the day I was born. He licked my full lips as I was lifted, and my legs wrapped around my favorite place.

"Shit, we need to be like Juniece and Lyric and get an open-air bath or at least one inside I agreed that is why we always chose their house for girls' night. They both had Japanese styled baths in their house. Shit, Lyric's was small but super cute of red and grey accents. While Juniece added a whole addition for a bath house with six bedrooms and her colors were purple, blue, silver and fuchsia.

"We do. Bae?" I yelped.

"Yes beautiful."

"No meals... we can't be late." I continued to say between them kisses he laid on me making me weak. Kano thought he was slick; my baby would eat my sweet peach for hours if I allowed him and unfortunately, we did not have that kind of time. He looked at me like I was crazy then smirked at me with those deep dimples that I loved so much.

"Bet. That goes the same for you, beautiful." Reality sat in as I pouted, poking my lip out for Kano to suck and bite on it with just enough pressure. The same way Kano loved my pussy is the same I loved his big, beautiful dick. I could suck it for hours and hours giggling a little thinking of that Muni Long song.

"Snack" we both suggested. Flipping in the sixty-nine positions, Kano went to feasting on my leaking kat like it was the sweetest peach of the season.

"Shh...hhhit daddy," I stuttered, putting me to shame with that tongue should have been illegal due to being so damn good Not wanting to be out done, I engulfed his dick down my warm hot throat, making sure he reached my tonsils. Five minutes later, we both screamed out in pleasure. I did have a big old belly in fact it was still flat, but I knew my baby didn't like his momma upside down, so we barely did this position in the shower. Placing on my feet, Kano bent me over and plunged in my gushiness until we reached our climaxed together. Tired and out of breath, we both did a quick shower and went to get ready. I attempted to grab my olive two piece set until Kano stopped me.

"Beautiful, we all are wearing the same shit in different colors because tonight's special. You gon match daddy's fly tonight." He handed me a bag from Suli, a store that was in our strip mall. They did custom clothes, and their suits and dresses were the best around. Going in the bag I saw it was a royal blue bandage dress that hugged my body right and tight and paired it with all black, red bottoms. I didn't do make up so most I did was a clear flavored blue berry lip gloss that Kano couldn't get enough of. I finished my outfit with my diamond stud and tennis bracelet with the matching neckless. Looking over, he sported a royal blue suit with a black collar shirt and black Gucci loafers with a black and gold Yacht master 42 Rolex.

"Damn beautiful you look good enough to drink ya bath water."

"Shit big daddy, I need to change this thong. You fine, fine." Kano gripped my ass as he licked the gloss on my lips before sticking his tongue in my throat. He pulled back and bent down going under my dress and removing the lace thong my juices wet up. After taking a whiff, he placed it in his suit jacket.

"Damn that pussy lethal. Let's go before I knock you up again." I giggled because I was already pregnant.

Later that night.......

When I say we looked good as fuck that's what I meant. Each of the couples had a color even though Juniece was by herself. She had on a burnt orange dress with matching heels. Chance and Lyric were sporting tan and white, while Nexus and Luka did black and red.

"Y'all thanks for supporting me and doing poetry night," Juniece cooed.

"Girl, we got you now go on up there before Chance get up in there like he did last time talking about gushy gushy. Matter fact where did he go?" Nexus asked.

"Oh, nell nawl. Lyric, your fine ass man up here again and you know he ain't got a lick of sense after he did that gushy poem then pulled out a gun on every nigga that looked your way. He ain't right!" the drag DJ Paula Deep yelled out, and the audience laughed.

"A P shut all that shit up this for all the niggas who go through shit like me. Tonight, my fine ass woman put me on punishment, so I dug up a poem for all my hurt. Baby I know you want to call me a brat, but I am your brat deal with that shit... Fellas if you understand me and know it say the anthem too."

"I would trade my life and all its riches
To rid my life of all the bitches

To watch a game just eating and drinking
To say, "Yo, get out my face," when she asks, "Baby, what you are thinking?"

To hang with my boys and not worry a bit
To get me a little ass and get on with my shit

To have a good life, baby, free from her friction
Barefoot, pregnant, and in the muthafuckan' kitchen

But hey, they got the booty now that's the hitch
And us without them, now ain't that a bitch."

This fool quoted the poem from *The Brothers* while Lyric had her head down embarrassed and all of us busted out laughing with his dramatic ass and all the men quoted that shit word for word. Chance was spoiled and it was Lyric's fault because she knew that he hated the words no or punishment.

"He makes me sick. I told him he was on punishment because he was going to make us late trying to keep having sex. He so damn spoiled man."

"Lil sis, you can't complain when he is putting all his energy into loving you. Didn't you have an issue when he was smiling in females faces?" Luka asked.

"Yea but."

"But nothing be happy with your man special ed and all," Luka Joked.

"Yea because not all of us are lucky enough to have that," Juniece said, getting up and going to the stage making us feel guilty in the process. She didn't want to move on; she wanted Demon and that seemed impossible. That hurt because we all knew she was lonely, so she poured all that into her kids.

"Boy, give me that mic you about dumb as hell. Sorry about my brother, he was dropped on the head as a teenager y'all. I never was a writer, but I wrote words on a page and somehow it was a poem to me. I fell in love with a boy who turned out to be my everything and just when it started it ended. Half of my heart died that day and even times when I think of him, I find it hard to breathe. I hope you enjoy this poem titled *"Someone I Love."*

"*I used to lay awake and dream what love will be like white picket fence, blue door, family of four funny how your plan is a joke to God's plan.*
I told him; this is the man I want, and he smiled & said this the man you need! Was he right? Yes indeed!
See I was scared and didn't know it and just like a poet he wrote a poem to my body that only he knew. Speaking Ebonics to a passage straight to my heart.
I had put up a wall it was very dark, but he knew that this journey was hard from the start. Those days when I felt ugly, he made me feel beautiful.
Those times I needed him and refused to speak; he took initiative himself.
The body I hate it he worshiped as if it was the finest piece of art to ever cross his path, he knew the secret, he found my laugh.

The moans the feeling like I was flying and could never fall each time we had sex was like I'm watching a movie it was always sensual Touching every part of my body even parts you couldn't see restoring my soul while defending my peace, boy you mean so much to me and all my years to one day be with someone I love To lie in his arms for me it was a dream that I never thought would come true, but oh boy even now I know the truth, so I will wait for the day our time will come and be there. Someone I love."

Devin

I'm coming home, I'm coming home
Tell the world I'm coming home
Let the rain wash away
All the pain of yesterday
I know my kingdom awaits
And they've forgiven my mistakes
I'm coming home, I'm coming home
...

Everyone clapped and busted out in tears, and I admit so did I. For eight long years' time stopped for her like it did for me. Coming home came through the speakers as Kano passed me the mic...

"There wasn't a time I didn't think of you.
Most days, I craved you wanted to embrace you, even pick up the phone and call just to see your face, hoping nobody filled my place. I watched you from afar, was so proud of your biggest moments that when you'd cry it'd make me question why. You were like discovering new territory; I wanted to enrich your soil and build to something new, yet this was foreign to me.

When I lose my way and trust I will, lead me back to you when there's something I'm not sure of, teach me so I'm giving you every bit of love you deserve and when I'm pushing you away, grab me and let me know that you're here to stay. Let me discover you."

"Whose voice is that?" Juniece asked, confused and frantic.

"It's, okay, gorgeous, you've heard this voice plenty of times, Juicy booty. Remember when I was ten, and my stomach rumbled, I hadn't eaten all day, and you gave me all your lunch. The teachers never noticed but your nosey ass did even when I was too weak to lift the sandwich to my mouth. You fed me and when I was done, you wiped my mouth and planted my first kiss on my lips. Damn, gorgeous, even then the sweetest kiss you gave had so much love how could I not notice you. So instead of hurting you, I waited and prepared myself to be all that you needed me to be, so you won't be runner up to no body. You were my first kiss and a lot of other things, and I understand that it hurt you, but you also have to understand you will be my last everything, but back to that day you remember what you said?"

"Yea, I do," she responded, still with silent tears while looking around.

"What you say, gorgeous?"

"I…III…"

"It's okay, listen to my voice. What did I say?"

"I said, I protect you until you can protect yourself, and I'd cover you whenever you were too cold. I will be your everything even when you have nothing. I will make you love me, and I will be your wife. Oh my God, I thought you forgot Juniece whispered, all choked up.

"Eight years, two months, four days, and as if it was yesterday, I want to discover you. Did you know you are my dream girl? I used to ask myself how did I get so lucky? So how could you know that I'd fight through heaven and hell to ask you, Juniece "Juicy" Mills wills you become my wife and forever friend until the end of time."

"Awwww," the audience cheered as my wife looked for me, so I stepped in the light matching her fly and she fell to her knees crying with her head down. I wasn't the same. She knew I changed in a way others would not understand. I had a burnt orange suit with a white shirt with three buttons undone and white loafers. Walking on the stage, I bent down and cupped her chin, staring in her deep brown eyes “Daddy’s home now, beautiful,” I whispered before kissing her like my life depended on it. Truthfully, it did and when I was done, I slid the ring on her finger without waiting for a reply. I lifted Juicy Booty up and carried her out.

“Where are we going? Our friends are in the VIP,” she said above a whisper.

“Eight years is a long time; they will understand. We got some making up to do.”

“Where are my kids?”

“With Mom until the dance on Friday,” she responded. I nodded my head. I was going to repair my family and hope they forgave me.

Juniece

This couldn't be real; he was here he was alive in my very presence and boy did I miss this man. I wanted to let everybody have their moment because they missed them just like I did but call me selfish, I needed him with candles lit throughout the bathhouse. Thank God Momma had the kids for the next two days because I wanted this time for us to love on each other. The school dance was Friday and me and Kano volunteered.

First, we used soap, scrubbing our bodies and the wash buckets to pre clean ourselves and scrub each other's back, not even saying anything just appreciating a moment for what it was. After a while, I was afraid to even blink to think maybe this was a dream, but it wasn't. I always made a promise to myself if I ever had a second chance, I would show him all the things that make him special. Standing us up I grabbed his hand and let him to the beautifully crafted Jetted pool.

Facing him, I stared at his eyes, and I leaned in for kiss. He stuck his tongue in my mouth and I sucked on it, cherishing the mint flavor, and weed that I found refreshing. I pulled into his embrace as he got acquainted with the body that had changed over the years. No, I wasn't your big girl that thought she wasn't good enough. I wasn't the skinny girl either who thought she looked too good to humble herself. I went from being a size twenty to a size fourteen. I still had curves, I had a flat stomach, my ass was still fat, and I had a breast reduction. Healthwise, them bitches were strangling me while I was sleep, but my thirty- four C's was still pumping juicy enough to feel his mouth and that's exactly what he did is he took my nipple and sucked on it while he played with the other. I moaned out in ecstasy. It had been eight years since a man touch me and baby, I was missing every part of a man's touch and my body reacted while I was still somewhat shocked. In my heart, I knew that he'd come back to me, and it would never allow me to move on.

"I'm not going anywhere, beautiful"

"You promise?"

"I spent eight years of not being able to be in your face or get on your nerves and love on all of you now until eternity, you have me until we take our last breath together because baby at this point, I want to die with you. Releasing my hair, I fell to the bottom of my back, and I gasp as he entered me. Ten thick, long inches slowly invaded my peach, ripping me like I was a virginally over again. I hadn't had sex in years, but I gripped his hips tighter, pumping slowly as he marked up my neck, and I bit my lips with tears still falling.

"Oh God, this is so good."
"You missed me, Juniece?"

"Yes. Yes. Yes. Yessss. I'm cumming ."

"Go head, lil mama. I am too." I dipped all on the pipe that punished my peach and he pumped releasing all his seeds inside me. For the remainder of the night, we had sex throughout the house, in every room not missing a beat. I fell asleep peacefully; I closed my eyes thanking the Father Almighty because without Him I wouldn't have had a man hand crafted for only me.

****

10 am

"Damn, Juicy I missed your cooking," Demon said, scarfing down the grits, egg, bacon with French toast I made. Truthfully, I miss cooking for him. I never really realized the things I missed until he came back. I guess I was numb to it all. It was the little things like nibbling on my ear and giving me back rides when we went on long walks or even washing my hair when we were in the shower. I couldn't believe he cut his dreads and let his hair naturally grow out, the long thick wavy mane adorned his face and what really took me by surprise was the tattoo he got over his chest with a lock and under it saying property of Juniece "Juicy Booty"

Mills. He was perfect and still I had questions about where he had been, but I didn't want to fuck up the moment.

"What I'm about to say can't leave out this room. I can't tell you how to feel, but I also need you to understand."

"Okay."

"After my parents died, and I started living with you and Ma, I along with Kano, Chance, and Luka made a deal with a very powerful family doing some bad shit and in return, they would give me the money to lay the groundwork for Phantasia. When I agreed to the deal, I was with Jesscenda. She was easy to leave, you, however I swear that shit would have been hard to bear. Then, we started being opened to our feelings and seeing you at my casket broke me."

"But you did leave. I couldn't eat, sleep, most mornings I was too sick to move, trying to process the events happening and that whore you were with left Devina in the walkway of our old home with shit up her back at only five days old. Lawd knows if I wasn't walking what could have happened," I said through clenched teeth mad as hell because Jesscenda would never change and would always find herself on the short end of the stick. I thought as I recalled that day.

"Jesscenda, what the fuck? Why would you leave the baby outside my door? What if I wasn't walking up just now?"

"She's not Duke's. He gave me a choice him or her."

"Let me guess you chose him? You're such a sorry excuse for a woman. You carried this beautiful child and like yesterday's trash, you're throwing her away."

"So, what, I deserve happiness. You got Demon and all that came with his love and what did I get, nothing but heartbreak, broken promises, and lies. I hated you, hell I still do because for the likes on me, I can't understand why he chose you. But she looks like him and if you don't take her, I will leave her on the steps of CFSA. You love him too much to let his child go in the system." Jesscenda scoffed. Taking in her appearance, she looked disheveled and as much as I want to beat her sorry ass, life had already taken a toll on her ass.

"Come in so we can talk first." Weighing her options, she followed me. I placed the baby down in the bassinet I put together for this baby shower I was throwing and went in the kitchen and grabbed wine and glasses, placing them in front of us and laughed out of nowhere.

"What's so damn funny?"

"You. When Devin was with you, I used to think why her? The same way you're doing now. I would be his everything except one thing I wanted, and I used to be jealous, but damn I was stupid. You thought it was our weight that separated us and made you more superior, but honey you are so wrong and so was I. You, bitch, are trash. I could never be with a man that can't love a child

that I carried and birth, not that you put up a fight all for love, huh. Of course, he chose me, I would never do the things you had done for the so-called love. Did you name the baby?"

"No."

"I will have my lawyer draw up documents giving me full custody. I will allow four visitations her whole life those ages will be between five and six because unlike you, I have a heart but know that I don't trust you, so I want to wait until she's of talking age."

"Bitch, I wouldn't hurt my child."

"This coming from the conniving hoe trying to leave her newborn on the porch." I shot back as she jumped up, attempting to slapped me as the baby began to cry. Her wails filled the room. Staring her in the face, "Hoe I wish the fuck you would with your basic ass. Now get your raggedy ass out my house, my daughter is crying I spoke with venom in my voice, then finished off my glass of wine. I picked her up and rocked her and her cries subsided. She was truly divine.

"Momma got the baby, and I promise to love you and protect you with all my heart. From now on you name will be Devina Justice Coles.

"Baby I know all that and yes, I have regrets, but I'm not apologizing for being able to provide for my wife and kids. I knew there was a chance that you might not forgive, maybe hate me, but Juniece you are my home, my person. No matter what I will fight the gods themselves to come home to you." I thought about the time had passed, and I had to ask myself could I forgive and live without him, and the truth was no. There were woman wanting this type of loyalty and love, and I had it.

"First let me tell you about our beautiful kids. Devina, our oldest, is smart and got a little attitude. She's infatuated with all things you. They both are. Ja'sai is nosey and energetic. They are extremely close and very spoiled. We took a family trip to Japan two years ago and fell in love with the culture and now for Vina birthday, she want a cosplay birthday party. So, we are throwing it at the Vineyard Phantasia just bought and of course, MA spoils them both. MA said when Vina mad, she looks like you. Despite all that's happen, I can't help but thank you for blessing me with these two amazing kids."

"I'm just thankful for being who you are."

"Let's play the Play Station?"

"Did you get any better?"

"I mean... I can handle do a little something," I replied, lying my as off and giggling.

"Lying ass. Come on let's go," he replied. I jumped on his back as we ran to the game room and for the remainder of the day, I had my best friend back. I told him stories about the kids, picture we had taken, and the videos we had made over the years and because he didn't want any secrets, he told me about Styx. First, I wanted to kick his ass because I hadn't entertained not one damn man. Then, I wanted to be petty but as a woman there's a question I needed to ask. I pulled away, and his grip became tighter.

"Where are you going, bruh?"

"You just keep hurting me. While you were gone, I never entertained anyone or looked at another man, but you couldn't keep your dick in your pants, but you love me, right?" I began tearing up and taking off the ring that was just placed on my finger hours before Devin stopped me grabbing my neck and tilting my head back to stare me in the eyes.

"Juniece, stop fucking playing with me. Don't get fucked up. I admit I was wrong, but I'm never going to let you hear no foul shit from nobody other than me. I'll never have you looking foolish, ma."

"You don't get it, growing up I had to watch you be with other bitches warming my spot and now you added one more bitch to the roster. How would you feel if I go fuck a nigga six times and say it didn't mean shit," I threatened?

"Juniece, I swear bruhh you fuckin trying me. Your ass spoiled and that shit's my fault, but when I asked you to marry me, and you didn't say no that meant we take each other's bullshit. Walk away from me, and I'll will kill that ass because there isn't no life without you. I'm sorry, ma."

Tears poured out, and Devin kept kissing them away. Thirty minutes later, I was all cried out, and I finally came to the realization that a bitch didn't wanna die when I loved this man and all his bullshit and being without Devin was death, so again I didn't want to die.

Nexus

Devin was alive and we were overjoyed watching the events play out, and to say we were shocked was an understatement. The only thing that didn't make sense was the fact that men wasn't surprised to say the least. They were quiet. Too damn quiet and the women all picked up on It.

"So y'all knew, huh?" I asked, irritated yet none of them said anything.

"So where was he after all this time?" Lyric ask.

"Y'all owe us something. For eight years, we watched our friend in agony and cry over a man for eight long years while we were moving on and y'all looking hella shady right now!" Drita snapped.

"There are things we can't explain, and we are damn sure not going to and put our family in danger. So let our friend's figure that shit out for themselves," Kano suggested. He was right though, the one who needed answers wasn't us. He was our brother, and we were just happy to have him back. After another hour of chilling and laughing having couples time, we all said our goodbyes and headed home.

Now y'all know ya girl been working her ass off by graduating with a culinary arts degree and cannabis business with a minor in cannabis extraction and manufacturing. I grew the best cannabis in the ten surrounding states all while still raising my siblings, and I will admit at first, I thought I made a mistake taking custody, but I couldn't imagine my life without them. First Luka and I got them into therapy because let's face it, my mom fucked us up, and we couldn't build a healthy relationship because of that so we all did family therapy as well to learn to talk and understand each other. Luka and I also owned a cigar lounge that you had to be invited to and the memberships ran between eight to twelve grand a month.

Before I knew it, we were pulling up to our house and I had the sudden urge to puke my lungs up in the powder room near our entryway. Going into action, Luka pulled my hair out the way.

"Bae, I told you to stop eating hot food. It is giving the baby heartburn," Luka scolded.

That's right we were expecting, and I still had a little pudge for a stomach, but nobody really noticed unless they see me with my clothes off. I was six months pregnant, and we were keeping it a secret until we were out of the woods. Over the years we tried, and I always ended up miscarrying. I kept worrying and stressing myself out so bad that it took my husband to tell me if kids will come. After Devin ass died, we had a small ceremony in our back yard, and it was truly the best decision I ever made.

"I know, bae but that's all I want to eat," I cooed while brushing my teeth.

"Not you tryna sound sexy with throw up breath."

"Bae," I whined.

"I'm playing Butt. How long we got before the kids get back?" he asked in a seductive tone.

"They at ya momma's house with the other kids so we got the whole house to ourselves. Shit, babe I'm getting extremely hot the dress feels tighter somehow," I whined.

"Calm down Butt," Luka said in that deep, sultry baritone voice I loved so much. Wrapping his around me, he ripped my dress down the middle in the back. "Feel better?"

"Yes bae, thank you."

"I'm the good guy now reward papi for being so nice."

Stepping out my dress, I got on my knees, releasing the monster, and swallowing all twelve inches before me. Luka had the biggest, sweetest, prettiest chocolate dick I ever saw and the only bitch that could handle Willy Wonka but me. I twisted and suck 'til he was ready to explode and like a kid waiting for a treat, I ate it all.

"Damn, do that shit with your nasty ass." Luka groaned, slapping me on my nice round apple bottom. Lowering myself on, we both moaned in ecstasy. Gripping my hips, Luka plunged in my dripping pussy repeatedly without remorse. Sex with this man turned me and him to different people and that was okay 'cause I loved all of that shit.

"Harder, muthafucka, tear this pussy up!" I yelled as Luka stood up, working his was throughout our foyer.

"OH, my dirty little slut you fucking back. Who taught you how to take dick like this?" Luka moaned between breaths, digging deeper in my guts, going in circles between squats and standing up.

"You did."

"What you say, Butt? Answer me, you know I love your voice."

"YOU DID, PAPI. FUCK YOUR DIRTY LITTLE SLUT!" I screamed and a dish dropped to the floor. Turning around to see Lee'Andra? Nyla, and Nate with their mouth wide open. We rushed behind the couch and grabbed the throw blankets laid on them.

"So, who's a dirty little slut?" Nyla teased.

"Nyla, hush child before I whoop your little ass.

Nate needs to talk to you and Luka."

"Okay give us a few minutes to handle our hygiene and find some clothes and we will be down to talk, Nugget." Rushing in our bedroom, Luka and I showered on each end of our dual shower as quick as we could. I threw on some of Luka's basketball shorts and then I put on anall -black sports bra. When we got back everyone was sitting at the table, including one we didn't know. "Ma, who is this?"

"I don't know honestly. I caught Nugget sneaking her in."

"Nate, you lost your mind. Why would you do something so damn stupid?" Luka barked. Nate knew better anyone who came on the property had to be vetted thoroughly because we took our family seriously.

"I know it was wrong, and I am so sorry, Nanna Lee, for being sneaky and not coming to you I the first place."

"It's okay baby. I know your heart but it's time you man up and tell your sister what's been going on with you, baby," Lee scolded and pulled him in a hug.

"I'm sorry for the mess I made tonight. Nate was trying to help me, and he done more than enough," the girl said as she turned to leave. I saw the bumps that went up and down her arm.

"Wait." I stopped her.

"You ever had chicken pox before?"

"Yes, when I was younger," she responded shyly.

"Are you in pain of any kind?"

"NO," she quickly said, but I could tell she was lying because shingles wasn't for the lighthearted. They were tiny bumps, yet they were painful as hell.

"I hate liars so make that your last one. Shit down while I get the first aid kit and then we will go from there, but you will tell me why my brother is risking so much for you," I suggested then she looked to Nate who nodded his head, letting her know it was okay.

"My mom died a year ago in the drug overdose over on 13th Street. We didn't have much nor did I have any family to rely on. Most days, I went to school just so I could have something to eat and turn in homework. For the past year, I've been sleeping outside because who wants to be in the system. I already know the horror stories when I was taken from my mom years ago. Nate saw me one night with practice was over and asked me was okay. I didn't want him involved how could he rescue me? He didn't owe me, and I was too scared to trust that he could help me, so I told him I was I was just waiting on my ride. A few hours later, I was still in that spot begging for change and embarrassed when he walked back up on me. It wasn't a secret I stink, but my education means something to me, and I couldn't let it go. I took bullying and pretended not to hear the jokes and as bad as I wanted to cry; what use would that do? Eventually, I gave in because he wouldn't let up so for the past three months, Nate has been sneaking me in the pool house to stay and tonight, he had told me that they will be staying at their grandmother's house, so I had to wait until he let me on the property. The deal if he helped me is I was never to initially ask for the code, he will provide me with clothes and food until we figured out something. Then, we got caught and you're not obligated to take care of me. I know I must go, and I appreciate the help so please don't be mad that he helped me," she announced before getting up to leave.

"Sweetheart, why didn't you ask for help or go to your teachers? They would have done something, called child protective services," Ma asked.

Nate slammed his fist on the table furious at Ma's suggestion. I couldn't understand why the girl was truly beautiful even with the bumps that she had on her arms. I had noticed she had on a marvel shirt that I had that Nyla borrow and it fit her little bit better.

"Come on, sis, you know what happens in the system. Hell, we wouldn't even in the system and look what happened to us. I couldn't let her be thrown to the wolves," Nate expressed in a saddened tone.

Lyric and I never had to experience that and the stories I heard from my siblings about the things that went on in those group homes made my heart hurt, and I wanted to help and from the look in Nate's eyes he had some sort of feelings for her. So, helping my brother was no option.

"So let me ask this, Nugget, are you asking me and your sister to help her because you genuinely feel something for her as a friend?"

"Bro, I'd never lie to you. I like her, but this is more to help a friend and I haven't done anything under either roof or outside this house for that matter. We don't want to confuse things. Down the line if it happens I will aways ask the brothers on the situation, but right now this is all I got."

"I must go, your father wants to talk about lord knows what. Don't make that face, son, my business is my business," Lee announced.

"God, forbid you deny the great Dola Musa. Don't you hate being his doormat?" Luka said, aggravated. Anytime it came to his parents, it was a touchy subject. Witnessing the arguments and the hurt his mother felt from all the broken promises, he was a child all over again, who didn't understand that relationships was complicated.

"Son, don't you ever disrespect me again in your life. I have never been, nor will I ever be any one's doormat. Now I might have left your father because he wouldn't lose his wives, but my let me sprinkle some knowledge on you. When we married, I graduated college with not an ounce of debt and built my career despite your father's wishes and even though I refuse to take anything from him, money is constantly added to that bank account that I still have yet to touch. Bills is paid for and it's not with my money. The only thing I use your father for is his third leg and even that is on my terms, so he makes appointments like my clients. I'm grown, and son you don't need to protect me. Stop making my issues yours and deal with the issues you have with your own father. His other wives might need him, but Lee'Andra Musa doesn't, now if you will excuse me I'mma let him scratch this itch before your new daddy be someone younger than you," Lee stated and left without a goodbye.

"She told you," I teased.

"Shut your ass up." Luka softly pushed me, walking away as I busted out laughing because he was a spoiled lil momma's baby.

"Why didn't you tell your mom that when she checked your ass? Nyla and Nate, go get you showers, and I want to have a talk with..."

"Jayda Collins."

"It's okay, Nugget trust me."

"Come on, Twin, trust our sister." Nyla pulled him away.

"Your home is beautiful," she nervously said.

"Thank you. There's no need to be nervous. My Nugget wants to protect you, so I will make you are long as you follow my rules and don't abuse his kindness because then it's all fair game, understand? You can stay in one of the spare bedrooms and continue to do great in school. I If you don't mind me asking, how you can afford to go to Galveston Prep?"

"I got in on a scholarship, and I've always maintained a 4.2 grade point average."

"And they've never said anything to you or stop the bullies?"

"Miss Nexus, they only care about grades and tuition and if those are appropriate, they look the other way. Your brother is a great guy, but I'm not ready nor do I understand what he wants from me. I don't even know what I want for myself."

"And the more you approach situations head -on, the clearer things will become. For now, let's get these shingles cleared up and make some appointments. We aren't here to judge you. We got you from here on out," I reassured her and pulled her in my embrace as she wept. I could have easily set her up on the family properties, but she didn't need that. This girl was alone and needed family and despite not knowing her, I trusted my Nugget.

Nate was excelling in his grades and great on a football field; he had grown so much. I was proud of him because after hearing everything that happened in his childhood, I was afraid he would cut the whole world out and go through it by himself, but every day he tried and opening himself up to be better than he was yesterday. Nate and Luka had a great relationship, almost close as ever. I appreciate that man because even when we down, people always have my back. Nala likes to stay closed off, and I wanted to get my baby sister out of the mentality that everybody is going to leave so when we argue, I lock in the root of the problem that she didn't have to go through it by herself, and I gotta remind her by holding her and repeatedly saying I got you because I did, now that I needed to stop bitches from trying her. She stayed getting in fights because my little sister was pretty, light skin, tall, slender frame. She didn't fuck with people because like Drake said, "No new friends." She was family oriented and had a mind of her own.

Nyla

16 years old

"Bitch, you got one more time to be in my man's face. Don't you smell my sweet ass pussy on his beard? Have some damn respect, we damn near married!" Keisha yelled.

Keisha was the captain of the cheerleading squad. She hated me since I stepped in this school, and I had no idea why Everyone knew she was embarrassed that Nate turned her down, but that was not because of me. He had a type, and he absolutely loathed bitches. My life was fucked -up enough, and I was nowhere near interested in her boyfriend, who she called damn near her husband. I will say this if it wasn't for my sister and Luka, I don't know where me and my brother would be. Of course, we started therapy. Lord knows we needed it, and I still attended because it was helpful. My sister also put us in things that we were interested in. In return, I learned to forgive my mom because if I didn't, I would destroy myself and she would win. There were so many nights my sister had to run in my room and rock me, reassuring me that things would be okay. Nexus put us first and anytime I was in trouble, her or any other family member were right there. They all knew about Keisha, but last week her nasty infested ass tried to flirt with Chance, and Lyric was outside telling her to get her momma so she could whoop both of their funky asses. Nobody wanted her man.

It had been three months since Jayda came to live with us, and she was becoming my best friend, and who knew the girl had skills. She could dance her ass off. We started taking ballet and Hip Hop and eventually, started doing ballroom dance with the famous Heart sisters and if you don't know who that is maybe you should read *Mistletoe's Hood love with a Bow.* It was fun. When I'm out there none of my problems mattered, I could soar as high as I want to stretch to the nearest land that I want to and be whoever I wanted to be. When I dance, no one could touch me. Yeah, here I was listening to this bitch go back and forth and one thing my sister taught me was never to be nobody's punk. Of course, I could have whooped her ass but what would it do? She was insecure, and I just wasn't in a business where I put energy into females like her.

"Keisha, I don't want your man. I don't entertain him when he talks to me, I don't know how you got my number, and I damn sure ain't scared of you. Please step aside and check the person you need to, ya man, who your damn near married to. Have a good day," I said, loud enough for only her to hear.

I wasn't trying to embarrass her or make an audience even though that's what she tried to do to me. Now I wasn't ugly by a long shot. I was like pretty for sure; I had long hair and a nice thin frame. I had a little breast that was a mouthful, but I had a nice little booty on me too, so it wasn't rare that boys always approached me but none of them knew me or wanted to know the real me. Like I said, I was fucked -up. I had issues and I was not about to let nobody add more on my plate than I could carry. When class was over, I met up with my brother at our car my sister gave us for our report cards being good. After ten minutes, my brother had yet to show up, and then I had in a text alerting me that he was still in football practice. He'd get somebody to drop him off at my dance class when it was over. After meeting up with Jayda, I pulled off while listening to Lotto's Bitch *Bitch from the Souf rapping* line-for -line like I was the bitch in charge. People said that I resembled TI's daughter, Deja but with a bigger butt, but I didn't see it. As soon as I got to my dance class, Ye'ar was there already warming up. He was a boy I was often fascinated with. He had a crush on me, and I was too scared to even take it there. He was from Japan and grew up with adoptive Black parents and his swag was out this world. He had the perfect V in his stomach with nice long hair, tattoos, and eyes that could make me weak with a deep sexy, sultry voice.

"Okay for the hip hop/ contemporary number let's do Jayda, Nyla, and Ya'er and Braden. Get in position. On the eight count," Blair ordered. I was paired with Braden while Jayda was with Ya'er and as cute as we looked, something still felt off.

"Maybe it should be a duet, bae. I like Ya'er and instead of Jayda lets pair him with Nyla. Cue music."

Can I call you baby? Can you be my friend?
Can you be my lover up until the very end?
Let me show you love, oh, no pretend
Stick by my side even when the world is caving in, yeah

"Nyla, you're infatuated with him. Every time he touches your face, you clam up. Part of liking a person requires seduction and right now you're giving me 'I gotta shit vibes,'" Christmas whispered.

"It's hard."

"It's not, though. Come dance with be. Everyone let's take fifteen." It was just Holiday and me. "When I met my husband, he was a whole sneaky link, and we met when we were teaching his sister bridal party ballroom dance."

"You didn't want to date him?"

"No that wasn't it. I had my own insecurities and issues that I didn't want to force him to deal with. We as women do that, making things complicated. You don't have to put a name on things, sometimes you should just go with the flow and let the chips fall where they may."

"And what if he doesn't like me like that?"

"I'm possible."

“How about today we work on the confidence in dancing, girls only, and you spend the weekend getting to know your dance partner. You can’t fake chemistry and unfortunately, that’s what is required.” For the remainder of the day, the girls went over the steps ‘til we had it down pact. When class was over, Jayda and I stayed to do our freelance. She was really my best bitch.

“Sis, I’m going to play the music, and I want attitude from the begging to end like when we in the dance studio. You been doubting yourself, and I don’t know why. Let’s fuck it up and leave no crumbs.” Megan Thee Stallion’s *Body* blasted through the speakers and like sis demanded, I dominated with her hitting every move with me.

Look at how I bodied that, ate it up and gave it back (ugh)
Yeah, you look good, but they still wanna know where Megan at (where Megan at?)
Saucy like a barbecue but you won't get your baby back

We were in our own worlds and when the song ended, I was sweaty, tired, and wanted to soak my bones and still keep dancing. Like I said, it made me feel free and invincible.

“Thanks, sissy.”

“Anytime I’ll always be there for you. Let’s go home.” We walked outside, and Nate and Ya’er were chopping it up.

"How was practice?" Nate asked, looking at Jayda. It was obvious they liked each other and were dating, yet neither of them wanted to put a label it.

"It was good."

"And yours, Jay baby?"

"Tiring, but I can't walk another step, Poppo." Turning around, Jayda hopped on my brothers back as he carried her to the car leaving me to talk with Ya'er.

"What was up with you earlier?"

"I don't know whenever we are paired up, I get self-conscious and doubt myself. Ya'er, I think you should dance," I suggested, disappointing myself.

"Nah that don't work, you're afraid but shit, I'll fix that. This whole time you been dancing and grinding on all of them niggas, I ain't say shit but now I'm marking my territory," he said, pulling me in his embrace. He kissed me without any remorse then trailed kisses to my neck and left a big ass hickey. "Since we met, you act timid around me, and I can't understand why. I don't entertain other females because I see only you and when you ready to be brave, come and find your savage, bae. I'll be waiting," Ya'er spoke before he swaggered away. Now I was still a nervous wreck, but that man walked away like he had a mongoose between his leg. I thought the stereotype was Japanese me had little dick and now I wondered ole boy's secrets.

Jesscenda

"So that's how it is, Duke? You're going to throw away your whole family for that whore. The last six years meant nothing to you?"

"Jesscenda, what we had was good. I love my kids, and I want to see them. I just can't be with you no more. Somewhere along the way, I just fell in love with her and being with you don't even feel right no more."

"I gave up my child to be with you. I gave you three kids after that. I have loved you and been faithful this whole time .and this is what you do. At least if Devin was here, he would have never done me the way you have!" I screamed as rage filled me. I wasn't perfect. I wanted love and yeah, envy got me in situations I should have walked away from, but I'd changed a lot. I thought it was different with Duke.

"It's always about that nigga, huh. You were always jealous of the best friend and coming in second place. You even had me telling you how much I loved you and how you wanted to be with me but because my pockets weren't as deep as your precious Devin's, you couldn't acknowledge a nigga, now he dead and gone, you were all willing to love me and sacrifice and do shit for me. Look, sign the divorce papers, Jesscenda, and let me go. In life, you don't always get what you want."

"What hurts is that you moved on to the closest person to me, knowing that was the only person I had in this world next to my kids and betrayed your so-called brother. You're a snake, and you're a coward, and I'm done crying tears over you, and FYI in case you haven't heard, I guess hell didn't want him because Devin's back. With your punk ass!" I screamed, yelling into the phone at Duke. My life was unraveling, and I was quickly drowning, trying to keep my head above water.

I watched the video over one hundred times, replaying it back-to-back, and I couldn't believe it. My baby daddy was alive and in flesh, and my blood boiled as I saw him propose to this fat bitch and say all the things, I wish he were saying to me. I couldn't help myself that I envied her. I was in love with Duke, and I thought he loved me too. It's funny how my life was completely falling apart, and this bitch was happy. Yeah, I gave up Davina. She wasn't for Duke, and I loved him more than I loved her sad to say. But reality came crashing down on our family a year ago after my cousin, Sia's husband, Mac died, things took a turn for the worst. She ended up moving with us because she was pregnant, and I wanted her to be okay sad to say, everything I have ever dished out to Fat Ass, I was paying for now.

Come to find out my cousin, the one I rode so hard for and vice versa, was sleeping with my husband in my bed and was pregnant with twins. Six months ago, he left me and his kids and said he was in love with her, leaving me with $60,000 and a note saying don't contact him. One thing about it when it came to my kids, I took very good care of them, but Davina being an exception. I wasn't crazy. I had a rainy-day fund that no one knew so we were going to be okay, but I needed a man to have all of me and this was my chance.

Over the years, my mom and dad and I worked on a relationship, and they would get the kids every other weekend. It was their time to have the kids, so I was thankful for that it was Friday night, and I knew they would be at the school dance because my oldest went to the same school she just went old enough for the dance yet and I knew all too well Demon was going to see his kids. Going in my closet, I grabbed a silver Gucci sequin dress and some silver pumps to go along with it then I ran in the bathroom handle my hygiene. When I was done, I beat my face to the gawds and place my hair in a messy bun and let a few curls fall loosely in my face, then I added some peach lip balm on my nice pump lips and headed to claim my man. After all those kids, my body always managed to bounce back, and I needed a shark to help me get revenge and be a family man at the same time.

Davina

I watched my sister and Uncle Kano dance on the floor to Dua Lipa's *Levitated,* and they looked like they were having a great time. I hated these dances because they always had a father and daughter's dance, and my daddy wasn't here. That was reserved for him, so I'd never dance. Ja'sai, however, loved dance for anyone who would watch and dance with whichever uncle who accompanied us that night. Tonight, was Uncle Kano's turn. I was just glad it wasn't Uncle Chance. He'd be over there dancing so hard that the girls be about to lose their minds over him, and the boys was too scared of Uncle Luka to approach us. I just really wanted my daddy.

I couldn't stand Jesscenda. She never got a chance to know me, nor did she want to understand me and love me. Some days, I wonder why I was even born. If it wasn't for my mom and my sister, I don't know where I would be; no that's not true because she said she loved me the moment my egg donor drops me off, and I truly appreciate her. She was my best friend next to my sister and my aunties. She tells us about our dad, never speaking on anybody negative even though Auntie lyric tells us all about my egg donor and how she came between Mom and Dad's love story and how Mom stood up to her but not the way she really wanted. We had been here for two hours, and the dance ended in another hour and a half and of course, it was almost time for the father and daughter dance. I wiped my hand down my face as a few girls from my class came over with their boyfriends in tow. Now before you say eight-year-old should not have a boyfriend, talk to them because Juniece Mills was not allowing nothing like that to go down.

"Poor Devina you don't have no daddy, you don't have no daddy," they chanted repeatedly. I been in this school since kindergarten, and they always teased me. The older I got, the more I couldn't ignore the things they said.

"I have a daddy. He just died that's all, he's in heaven looking down on me, loving me. You don't know anything about that. Crystal, why don't you just go over there and dance with your dad and leave me alone," I said just above a whisper, hoping to alarm Uncle Kano. I didn't want to interrupt him and Ja's dance. I might have been older, but Ja was the scrapper out both of us. I had fight I just believed that violence didn't solve anything.

"Just admit it your dad left to get a carton of milk because he was too disappointed in your ugly self," Crystal teased.

She always brought up the fact that my dad was nowhere to be around, yet her dad didn't even have a job, and he only showed up because her mother forced them to, and her boyfriend, Damon. his dad was no better than a rich slut. It was no secret that he stepped out on his marriage with a few of the teachers in the school. I used to have a crush on them until he said I was too black. Crystal was pretty. She was mixed with green eyes and long, sandy blonde hair. I, however, was brown skin with hazel eyes and medium length hair that stopped at my neck. I had my daddy's eyes and my mama's skin blemish free and thick plump lips. If anything, Jezebel gave me, it was lips to make a boy go crazy at least that's what my mama told me and with all those looks, it didn't stop the boys from teasing me and the fact they still called me ugly any chance they got.

"Bitch, why are you here with your ugly ass? Did you think I would ask you to dance or you going to dance with your uncle again because nobody loves you." Tears begin to block my vision. I shoved Damon so hard because he was so mean. Why couldn't they just leave me alone and let me be in peace. All I wanted to do was wish my dad was here but before I knew it, he reacted and slapped me across my face.

"Lil nigga, I know like fuck you didn't put your hands on my niece!" Uncle Kano yelled as the teachers ran to intercept him. They saw the situation and chose noy to do anything about it because I was just another Black kid on their roster.

"Sir you cannot be cussing at the students."

"You know what, fuck them little bastards. I ain't see your lil howdy doody ass come over here when they were teasing my mother fuckin niece. You know what, I got something special for that ass though. Ja' and Davina sit down. Give me twenty minutes, I got a surprise for both of y'all."

"I'm sorry, sir, but I might have to ask you to leave," the teachers said, trying to get Uncle Kano to leave, but he wasn't budging. He was adamant on his surprise, and I was smiling; something was telling me I was going to be smiling genuinely from now on.

"Listen, nigga, you might think your THNIC (the head nigga in charge) but you ain't. Tomorrow, I plan on buying this school because let's face it my family is the Black Thug Elite and when I sign those papers all you restarted racist muthafuckas is fired. Now take you ass over there and get that lil' niggas parents for the main event," Uncle Kano barked as Principal Downs ran away to follow orders.

"Say the word, Twin, and I will cut that hoe's hair," Ja'sai said, bouncing her leg. We weren't twins but it always felt like we were.

"What good would that do? Mahatma Gandhi once said be the change that you wish to see in the world."

"That all good, but what we are not going to be somebody's punk. You remember what Nanna told us a future queen never bow to peasants. In life, we are constantly evolving. Racism still exist and choosing to be peaceful will allow people to walk over you. Mommy always says that a person always have to fight to have a voice, but when are you going to let us hear yours."

"Sir, please calm down."

"You got ten seconds to move out my way," a voice that made us look at each other said. We hadn't heard that voice since we were kids. Tears began to fall because he couldn't be here.

Devin

"Bae, you ready?" Juniece asked, coming out the room Glowing

She had on a blue jean bra top and matching purse and shoes, which was paired black ripped jeans. She had her hair ironed bone straight with a middle part. Adding a black fedora hat with blazer, she was thick still just with a flat stomach, and I couldn't get enough of how fine she was. Wait let me take that back, Juniece was always fine, but she never had this type of confidence. I had to shift my dick in my pants because this was going to be a long ass night.

"Yea, damn you're so beautiful. Let's go get my kids before we make another one tonight.

"Thanks, daddy. We got time to make a whole damn basketball team." We hopped in Juicy's all white Range Rover and pulled off. Thirty minutes later, we were pulling up, and I was nervous as hell. Juniece placed her hand on mine.

"It's going okay, just like you we prayed for you to come back," Juniece reassured me as my phone lit up, indicating I had a text.

Kano: Aye, cuz at the school's father and daughter dance with your daughters. Get down here. I was going to handle the situation, but you waited eight years to do this. Lil panty thief boy smack your oldest baby.

"Bet. We are getting out now," I replied quickly read that text. had fire in my eyes.

I ain't even hit my kids and after missing years of that shit, I'd be damned if I let another muthafucka come in think they going to touch with belongs to me. I had dressed in the tan suit with a brown color shirt and brown Gucci loafers a Cuban Link in a Rolex. Just to set that shit off, Juicy had already braided my hair in two cornrows that made a nigga look good as fuck. Soon as I walked in, Kano was right there and this damn principal tried to ask a question like I gave a fuck.

"Where is the parents and the little boy that put his hand on my daughter?" I barked.

"Sir, please calm down."

"I pay too much money to this school for my kids to be treated fucked-up, there has been too many incidents to ignore. Get them out here now!" Juniece yelled.

I wrapped my arm around her waist and leaned into her ear. "Damn, I love it when your ass in control."

"Yes sir, right away." The principal left and came back with two funny looking parents and their dick yanking big headed ass kid. Now. I know that everyone thought I was dead, so all of them had questioning looks on their face but mine screamed don't test me, and I meant that shit. Before I knew it, the crowd was parting and slowing coming into view were the most beautiful kids I could have ever made.

"DADDY!" Devina and Ja'sai screamed, running into my arms. We cried and heard the joy in my kids' cries because they had their father. Most females would have moved on or would have been angry. Some would have even not taken Davina, but that's why there was only one Juniece in this world.

"Daddy, you can't ever leave. sissy can't take it. I'm a little thug but sissy well she needs a little more love than me because even though she doesn't think I know; she has cried for you. So, you got to promise okay," Ja'sai ordered.

"Daddy is home, I promise and what about you, Ja Ja do you miss Daddy?"

"Daddy, of course, but Sissy is my bestest friend, so I had to have her back and now that you're here, you can have ours and Mommy's back. Right now, be the dad Sissy needs. Good luck," Ja'sai said, walking into her mom's embrace.

"Ok Ja. Vina, baby, look at Daddy."

"No! I can't. Because if I open my eyes and you're not here, I don't think I'll survive. The kids stayed teasing me saying that I was too ugly for my dad to raise me and even though I know it not true, it hurts and when the dances always came, I would watch because you my daddy and for once, I wanted a parent to choose me that created me," Davina ranted and that shit hurt a nigga heart because of Jesscenda's actions, my baby was insecure and felt unwanted and that shit hurt. How could she not see that her mom, who wanted her was the best choice, and her dad was going to fix that. Grabbing Davina's face, I kissed a kiss on her forehead as tear silently fell from my eyes.

"Daddy is here and if you have to hold my hand and call me every hour until you understand and believe it I will, but right now I believe I owe my girls a dance with my wife." I started leading my family to the floor then turned around. "Give Daddy a minute to scare this lil' nigga and then I'm all your," I replied. When they were out my range, it was the principal, the fuck family, Kano, and me. I pulled my Glock from behind my back, and they looked mortified. Of course, I wasn't planning to shoot them, but I was going to scare the fuck outta this little nigga.

"So, you get off fucking with my daughter, huh?"

"Sir, wait," the father tried to speak up in a shaky voice before I stopped him.

"Nah ain't no wait. Just like that's your son, that is my beautiful ass daughter your son put his hands on. Now I'm aware your son is a child, so I'mma whoop you ass for not for raising this lil nigga to be a woman beater. I don't even hit my kids," I spoke through clenched teeth and started fucking ole boy up 'til he couldn't move and when I was done, the wife and the son was crying. I still wasn't satisfied, so I took off my belt and whoop the son. Then went to dance with my girls.

"Sir, wait," the principal stuttered.

"Nah, I've done enough of that. Kano handle that. My daughters want to dance with their daddy."

"I got you cuz."

"Follow me along with your woman beating ass son," I heard Kano start before the music drowned out his voice and Luther Vandross *Dance with My Father* came blasting through the speakers, and I danced and spun my kids all around the room. No this wasn't going to fix us overnight, but this first memory was a nice start. For the remainder of the dance nobody dared to interrupt us and for the first time in a long time, I thanked God for blessing me after I thought He gave up on me. Was it worth it? I asked myself would I do it again? And I could think was yes because of my moves. I tucked my kids in beds and noticed they didn't want for nothing, and gunshots didn't wake them out they sleep. They had the security that I wished I had when my parents were alive and that made everything worth it.

****

40 minutes later

The dance was over, and everyone was damn near gone. The girls were talking my head off as Juicy took it all in as we walked to the car. I was enjoying every minute of that shit though. Unlocking the door, Jesscenda walked up to me, placing a kiss on my lips. I pushed her dumb ass smooth off me.

"This bitch stay being disrespectful. I surprised it took her thirsty ass this long," Juniece expressed.

"What is she doing here?" Davina asked with so much hostility and hurt that I made me look at Jesscenda with a death stare.

"Davina, I'm your mother, acknowledge me and show respect."

"Hoe don't act brand knew you only birth her that is my daughter, and she don't owe you a damn thing. I was waiting for your desperate ass to pull some shit and you couldn't even wait a week before trying to look like you care," Juniece spewed.

I could tell she was pissed. After guiding Ja'sai in the car, I knew how this was about to play out, and I wanted my kids to be safe because the way shit was going down, my baby momma was about to be six feet under if she didn't get the fuck on with her sorry ass.

"Please, that's my daughter, Fat Ass, and despite what you think I love her and if you would let me see her then she would know that."

"Bitc..."

"Mom, let me get in the car with Ja," Davina said, stopping Juicy. "It took Dad to come back for you to acknowledge me. You had four visits, cancelled two and ignored me for your husband and kids during the others. Did you know I have abandonment issues because if you didn't love me to choose me, how can anyone else? Most days, I'm scared to be myself that my little sister protects me, my mom the one who is rides for me never waivers and never blames me for what you did. I am ashamed of you but most of all, I hate you because you don't deserve me. Your kids go to this school, and you pick them up, walk past me like I am invisible. I am not some bargains deal you can use as leverage to get a man that clearly don't want you. After today, I will never speak your name, but you will remember mine every time you realize that you are and idiot to think my dad will ever choose you over my dope, beautiful mom. You will never compare."

"You little ungrateful bitch...." I guided Davina in the car. As soon as I turned my back, Juniece went in throwing punches just like I taught her and don't be fooled because Juniece's punches hurt like shit. Jesscenda wasn't ready, she cried as she tried to block the hits coming her way. I was wrong for letting my girl beat my baby momma's ass, but this was long overdue.

"Stop, Demon, get her off of me!" Jesscenda yelled as if she was almost begging.

"Nah, hoe don't ask my man for shit with your basic ass. This was long overdue and you're lucky this ass whooping is all your getting you desperate, rabbit hole ass slut!" Juniece yelled ass Kano whistled, alerting us that people were coming out. I told him what was going down so he could run interference.

"Baby, we got to go she's barely moving, and my kids seen enough," I whispered, but Juniece kept swinging. I grabbed her and her ass tried to hit me. I caught her by her wrist. "Calm the fuck down, don't make me repeat myself again."

"She hurt my daughter; did you hear her?" Juniece began to cry.

"Yea and when we get home, we gon' talk and make shit clear that she doesn't have to feel that way ever again, but what I won't do is let her mother go to jail for this trash. I can handle a lot of things but losing you is not one of them.

After getting herself together, we went home. That night I made a promise to my kids; from here on Daddy was going to fix, repair, and restore. We cried, laughed, and watch anime all damn night and the shit was actually dope, but that damn Reincarnated as a slime was my shit. The dogs even took a liking to me but that damn Natsu and Gahjeel was going get their big ass whoop if they thought they was sleeping with my wife.

"For my birthday, I want everyone to dress up in my favorite anime characters," Davina announced. We were sitting on the couch with our pajamas, and damn it dawned on me... How could I miss this when I never had this? It was perfect. They were perfect.

"Oh yea? Who you want Daddy to be?"

"Rimaru and Mommy can be any girl in his harem?" she replied, serious as fuck.

"Harem? Davina, stop before your father blows a blood vessel."

"Okay but Daddy, you need to get hip," Davina and Ja'sai said at the time.

My girls were cute as fuck and resembled they momma with her fine ass and soon as night was done, I was gonna get into Juicy guts and make me a son.

Lee'Andra Musa

My son always thought he had to protect me from his father. Dola wasn't a bad guy, he just needed guidance that I wasn't willing to give him. In Nigeria, men are worshipped and treated like kings, and women are expected to cater that. My mother pushed for marriage and always told me it was my fault when we argued. A woman is supposed to follow and obey. That is what she did, and I was not her. I went to Penn State University in Pittsburgh on a full scholarship. The women there was so different than how I was raised, and the more I stayed the more I questioned what I wanted, still I married Dola and eventually, I fell for him because he was a great guy, but I was far too Americanized to allow myself to share him with another woman. At forty-six, I still could hold my own. Brown complexion, sepia eyes, round full lips, nice full tits, and a plump ass lets me know I was doing something right and there wasn't a man I couldn't have, but the one I wanted didn't just want me and that was the problem.

After leaving Luka's house, I went shopping and

then talked to Julissa and Brook while I cooked and talked about the men that stayed clouding our judgment. After we vented and planned our next couple of trips, events, and meetings, I showered and put my hair in a messy bun with some boy shorts and sports bra and went to the kitchen to pour me a glass of wine. It still bothered that Dola didn't show up three hours ago, nor did he call or text. He was grown and so was I, but I refuse to beg. I started walking to my bedroom when I heard my alarm being deactivated. Whoever it was had to be family because to get through the gate of the family estate. Two minutes later, I saw my husband walking to me with a faceless expression and tho suitcases and one duffle. One thing about thing man, he was fine and even whenever he pissed me off, he still made my pussy ache and cry for the thick stick between his legs.

"What are you doing here?"

"Well, hello to you my dear," Dola answered, ignoring my question which was too calm for my liking. Then, he grabbed my chin before sliding his tongue in my mouth and continued pulling his suitcases and duffle towards my room. "I'm going to shower then we can talk. I know it late, so I'll make it quick because you have work tomorrow."

I sipped on my wine quietly trying to wrap my mind around the bags that sat in the middle of my floor. After ten minutes, the bathroom door open with steam coming out with Dola having nothing but a towel around his waist. Dropping it to the floor, my eyes immediately went to his mid-section and like pieces to a puzzle falling into place the flood gates open, and I instantly became wet. His skin shined beautifully even with scars and bruises it still added to his appeal.

"What is all this about?" I asked, turning away from his serious gaze, never even bothering to cover up. He sat on the bed we have shared countless times over the years. Physically, I left him, but he always had the key to my heart.

"When I married you, I thought the ideals I had was of man, but they were not. I didn't deserve you and because it was forced on us, I betrayed you when you needed me most, I look for comfort by taking more woman and comparing them to you," he said, reaching out for me, but I moved away from his embrace. This was a little bit too late for that.

"Aht, aht I can't do this tonight. I waited. Waited years for you to say this while you were filling up a roster. You had me. Dola, why now? We have a good thing going between us. When you are here, we live in a fantasy and when you leave reality becomes... " I attempted to walk away before pulled me in his embrace. His scent invaded my nose.

"I've changed, Lee, and that fantasy can become reality. I was in Lagos having lunch with some friends, and they were talking about their wives being money hungry, competing kids, and utter chaos. Then, I thought about you and how driven you are, funny, sexy. I don't want my kids not to be ambitious and not to follow their dreams and be money hungry. Rayden wants to be around Luka, and I know that's up to him. I have been a fool. I told Mia, Gia, and Sophie that if it isn't involving my kids, there is no need to bother me because I want and need my wife. I want to build a relationship with my son and get to know the family you two have seemed to build. I want to be with you," Dola confessed, leaning in for a kiss, and I allowed him to.

Jumping up, I allowed the man who had my heart to carry me to the bed. Dola was a beautiful man; he could move you with his words but when we were intimate, the way that man spoke to my body was completely different. When we a woman of a certain age, the first thing we think to accept or ignore the situation. Women we deserve better, so be selfish and make demands because no matter the situation, you are worthy. I left on my terms, we had relations on my terms. And finally, I had him completely.

"One chance, ahhh," I whispered then gasped as his filled my insides with such sweet pleasure. For the rest of the night, I needed Dola to talk to me. I just hope Luka wasn't going to hate the idea of us and getting to know Rayden. Dola wasn't a small man, his dick was about ten inches and as wide a cucumber, and the last time we had sex was over seven months. I know I said I'd been dating, but no one made me feel like this man. Between the biting, sucking, and licking on my neck, I was going wild. Walking to the couch and sitting down, he ripped my robe open, taking my breast in his mouth as if he hadn't been eating.

"Ohhhh," I moaned out, riding Dola with no remorse.

"Shit, this pussy was meant to be handled roughly. Tell me Lee Baby, you want me to nice and ruff or you want tenderness, or do you want daddy to slut you out with no remorse?"

"I... want.... all... of ....it.... Fucked..." putting my weight on Dola's chest as he squatted and pumped with no remorse until I coated his big dick inside me and although it felt good, I was so happy I couldn't get pregnant. After cleaning each other off, we laid in the bed eating ice cream.

"Man, I miss being home."

"Great pussy will make you feel that way. But mess with my heart this time around, I'mma shoot you in ya dick after I screw you one last time."

"Why you don't love me. Me sexy, ain't it?"

"Maybe," I cooed.

"Come suck this dick for me."

"With pleasure, king," I replied to him, swallowing Dola whole. He taught me how to please him and like a student learning from a teacher the first time, I took notes. No one would ever be more than me to this man that's why it hurt to find out about his other wives because all together, they were a portion of me.

Julissa

"So here we are on this triple date and sneaking behind our kids' backs." Lee'Andra giggled.

She had been so happy these days since Dola was back in her life. We all knew he was the love of her life, but she refused to give into his terms and even though she thought it was selfish, my girl knew her worth. There were plenty of nights when she would go on dates and cry on the phone to Brook and me about how they wasn't Dola. We understood that all too well. Love didn't stop because we aged, and it damn sure didn't mean settle for anything. We deserved to have the love we watched our kids reach for and nothing less. Shit, I told Santino that I didn't want a star, nigga my pussy was worth a galaxy, and he said impossible, but if he couldn't make it happen, he was going to shoot Nasa for being incompetent. Y'all, if I knew anything I knew this marriage should be about the biggest, flashiest, richest anything. It should be about the connection you share with that person, the friendship you can't live without, the small things he thinks you don't notice, the no reason at all passion. Those I'll take over the *'I's married y'all"* ass bitches.

"Excuse you, Lee, my daughter knows about Santino and let's face it, that man be doing shit to my body that should be illegal. The other day, we went to his niece's quinceañera and fucked in the bathroom so hard that I had to put my thongs in his mouth to keep quiet. I haven't gotten them back yet."

"Okay so you are leaving your coochie juice all over the bathroom at a kid's party?" Lee asked.

"We judging now? Didn't you open them legs for daddy long strokes? I like the adventure though it feels good finding love on our terms."

"Well good luck with that, Silas keeps mine in this drawer at home for when I'm mad at him, and I swear the sex is amazing. But we all know Chance is a special case, that fool come out is he, his daddy. Just to be petty." We all giggled knowing it was the truth. When it came to his mom nobody was worthy. We all talked and laughed while placing dinner on the table. We had fried fish, greens, yams, chicken, cornbread, and red velvet cake that adorned the conversation.

"Dola, so what is your plans now?" Brooke asked while flirting and kissing on Silas.

"Honestly, just trying to show Lee the love she deserves the first time around and reconnect with my son. Spend some time in our home in Lagos and eat every part of her," he replied seductively.

"I thought you sold it."

"Lee baby that home has memories of us in it. I would never sell a place that brought such pleasure and love to my life. It was our first home," Dola stated matter of fact.

As we watch the two go back and forth, you would have thought they would fuck in front of us. Lee was nowhere near ugly, she resembled Porsche Williams from Housewives of Atlanta but with more sense 'cause if she ever did some hoe shit like that bitch did and fuck my man, she was catching all these hands, but she wasn't like that, so we were cool. Brook's freaky ass too. We were a sisterhood the day we met was the day we became sisters.

"Is it pretty?" brook ask Dola and Lee as they watched each other across the table.

"Ten bedrooms, twelve baths. Matter of fact, we should go for Thanksgiving, all of us," Dola invited.

"We in," Brook and Silas said in unison. They just didn't want to see Chance because he was so damn spoiled that Brook refused to tell him she was dating her first love from high school. I didn't know how they would deal with that.

"We down, right Mami."

"Of course, papi chulo," I cooed then leaned over to kiss him, spilling the wine on his shirt. "Papi, let's go clean that before it stains," I suggested, and Santino was on board because three seconds flat were in our bedroom, with me bent over while Tino rammed his nine-inch bat into my tight wet peach.

"Ummmm," I moaned out as this man pounded me without no remorse. Before I knew it was, I was cumming and so was Tino. After cleaning ourselves up, we went back like nothing happened. '*Grown Folks Business Holiday in Lagos coming soon.*

Chance

I had my reservations about Japan, but it grew on me. The culture was not only rich but refreshing on my relationship. By no means my girl was ever lazy but seeing her in her element and reinventing Japanese cuisine made me have a new take. I walked in the house looking for Lyric only to see her in her office at her desk with her back towards me. Shit, even I did better. I was creating my own line of quality Hennessy. Shit we were so busy that instead of having kids, we got a close friend's sister to be our surrogate and now we had another situation coming in seven short months.

"Arigato sensei." (Thank you, teacher.)

"Hontoni jojo-tekina im wa anata o totemo hokorini omotte imasu. (Really Lyric I'm super proud of you.)

"Arigato."

"Atarashī sake of happyō suru chansu wa dōdesu ka, soshite sore o anata no resutoran de toraedokoro no nai mono ni shitai to omoimasu. (How is Chance doing? I'm unveiling a new sake and would like it to be elusively in your restaurant)

"Kare wa sugoi. Soshite watashitachiha, raishū no owari made ni anata ni denwa o suru yō ni kare ni iu koto o nozonde imasu. (He is amazing. and we would love that I'll tell him to give you a call before the end of next week.)

"Daijōbu watashi no utsukushī minarai."
(Okay my beautiful apprentice.)

"Flitlrting o tsudzukete kudasai, soshite, tohru wa anata ni mukatte imasu. (Keep flitlrting and Tohru is going to get you)"

"Kono yoimono no subete o mitsukeru no wa muzukashīdesuga, sugu ni hanashimasu. Sayōnara (All this good stuff is hard to find but talk soon. Goodbye.)"

I watched Lyric from afar and honestly, I was amazed and proud of who she was ultimately becoming. Not only did my baby get a chance of a lifetime to study under Masaharu Morimotoand got into the university of Tokyo and dominating with a 4.2 GPA; between the business and the hours she put in to create foreign dishes that included cannabis. Lyric smiled as she finished up her call with Ken. He owned his own Japanese restaurant and his own sake company and truly became one of my best friends over there. Even though he was married, he always said Lyric was going to become his second wife. I honestly thought I was going to have to beat his ass. But it was all games, and his wife was close friends with us since we met her during their internship together. Taking a seat, I watched her saunter her fine ass onto my lap. She had a pair of my basketball shorts on with a sports bra and some all-black tennis shoes with her hair up in a messy bun, which let me know she needed my advice on something and the only way to do that was sex or basketball and since she was dressed up that meant she was stressing.

"You know I can always feel you staring at me."

"Do it make you nervous?"

"Honestly no," she replied, giving me a kiss before I tapped her on her leg to get up and go get dressed myself.

"Give me five minutes." After I dressed quickly, Lyric was bouncing the ball like she was meant for that shit. She dribbled the ball and shot a three, that shit was nothing but butter. She faced me dribbling the ball in front of me.

"First to five," she suggested. Nodding to confirm, I got my head in the game because my baby could ball with the best of them.

"When we were in in Japan, I saw something different in us. We were inspired. I had an idea but was scared the girls wouldn't back me and then I had a conversation with Gabby. She is flying in with Tohru and Ken," she said, biting her thick, soft lips.

"Lyric, baby you doubt yourself, and I can't understand why you know Japanese cuisine and you offered Tohru a chef job because she can cook her ass of at the inn while we deal with Gabby," I replied, doing a layup on that ass.

"How do I explain it all?"

"We, tell the truth. Our dreams were so big we put kids on the back burner and when we found out how difficult pregnancy would take on your body, we decided on a surrogate and then tell them the rest. They are your friends, sisters, and hold all your secrets. If you can't tell them your problems, then what are they here for?" I rambled. As tough as she was Lyric still doubted herself and stayed running from issues like I wouldn't catch her if she fell. She was my rib; without her I couldn't be me."

"I'm pregnant."

"I know."

"How." She giggled then had that gorgeous smile surface on her face. Damn, she was beautiful that I walked up with the ball in my hand, gripping her face and sliding my tongue in her mouth.

"Shit, I been up in that since high school, trust me Lil Bit. I know it all and before you ask, we gon make it work. Have faith in your husband."

"I always do."

"Then what you worried about? We got all these in-house nannies we might as well use them, and we can even ask Gabby to move in."

"Nah we good."

"Why, I thought you liked Gabby?" I asked. Gabby was Tohru's sister, and they never had an altercation and talked often so a nigga was a lil confused.

"I do and continue to do that after she delivers our twins, we will use Drita or Juniece's nannies because her unmarried ass is not going to be tempted to climb on my husband's dick."

"Bae, she not thinking about that."

"That's because when we chose her, and you left to go to the bathroom, I pulled out Marley and told her miracles come true, and she can be an angel real fucking quick," she replied serious as hell but shit like that turned me on. When she walked across that stage, I cried, when she said I do, I cried and when she promised that she'd protect a nigga heart, I damn for sure cried and not because I was a damn crybaby or bitch it's because after all the niggas I killed, I should have died a long time ago and this girl here no matter what the situation was, never let my hand go. I was lucky, maybe even blessed. Dropping the ball. I picked Lyric's sexy ass up as her legs went around my waist and arms went to my neck.

"Bae you wild. But nobody got my heart like your mean freaky ass. You the only person who saw my tears besides my momma so that mean when I look like a punk, you can't leave me."

"You my man, bae, and I'mma stick beside him," she joked, leaning down to kiss me. "There's nothing in this world I wouldn't do for you." She quoted the song by KeKe Wyatt, and that shit made a nigga feel good. I had a real one. Walking in the house, we joked then fucked real fucking nasty.

Jayda

Life for me was becoming clearer. In the beginning, I didn't understand what the idea of family meant but Nexus and Luka taking a chance on me meant the world to me. They didn't treat me different because I wasn't their blood instead, they embraced me; all the family did really. I called all the girls' sisters and all the boys' brothers, well everyone except Nate. Nyla and I were the closest. Though she knew all my secrets and knew all my thoughts, she even gave me advice when it came to fall in love with her brother which wasn't hard. Poppo is what I call them because most days, he thought he was my daddy, and he was just my friend. He wasn't even my boyfriend yet. But every day, he proved to me that there were no outs to this and that he would always be there for me. There were times females in a school would call me a charity case or little dirty birdy and as much as those hurt, they would be right there to defend me. It'd been six months since I started living with them and now, I understood what made woman that stood alongside the man so special. These relationships were not base without responsibility. They were nurtured and carefully thought through; the love that they created was nothing to be shy about, and I wanted that. The only thing I hated about it was the fact that the bitches in this school couldn't respect what we had, so of course I got in fights, and Nyla did too along with me. We had decided we wanted to be choreographers and professional dancers, and Nexus made us promise two years of college first, so of course we had a plan to do just that.

I stood in my closet with a towel on looking through my closet as Nate walked in my room with packages placing them on the bed. I slid on my bra and underwear then put on my uniform for work. The family owned a lot of businesses, so all the older kids rotated to earn extra money. which I had no problem doing. Luka and everyone else still put money in our accounts weekly. I wasn't blood, but I was family. Everything Nyla and Nate got, so did I and because I hated driving, my car sat in the driveway a lot, but I had no choice today because Nyla finally manned up and went to get Ya'er back. She was miserable, and she needed to stop doubting herself because my bish was bad all the way around.

"Hey Poppo."

"Hey, beautiful. What are you doing?"

"Getting ready for my shift."

"Come talk to me really quick."

Turning around, I saw him and was ready to give him all I could. Instead, I opted to just talk as he laid on my bed with his hand behind his head. I climbed on his lap and Nate gripped my ass. I leaned in and kissed him on his lips. We both told Nexus that we wanted to be together, and she dragged my butt to the doctors to get on birth control, not that we had sex yet. I wasn't ready to give myself completely, and I was glad he was willing to wait. We did however performed oral on each other and since he gon' be my last everything, I was satisfied taking it there.

"I left practice today and heard you and Lisa got into another fight. What were you thinking?" he scolded me, but shit I was tired of defending my place in his life.

"I was thinking I was tired of being bullied and people saying I secured the bag by becoming your in-house whore. Why do you think I refuse to drive to school?"

"I get that, but they don't have shit to lose you do. We all agreed to take advance classes so we could graduate early. And because we didn't trust many niggas, all of us was applying to the same colleges and was planning to get a four-bedroom house by the campus.

"I know, but I'm tired, Poppo," I whined. He hated they teased me, but he also wanted me to stand on my own, but they would have to be after school business.

"I know, bae. The world is filled with niggas who gon say shit they know nothing about, but the only one that should matter. It got you and you better have me."

"Without question, Poppo."

"That's right, lil mama." He always made me feel better. In his presence I was special, and in his eyes, I was perfectly imperfect. Looking down, I saw that Nexus was calling me.

"Hey sis, I am about to leave in ten minutes," I rambled off because one thing Nexus hated was us being late.

"You don't have to come in today. I switched your schedule because Nomi can on fit you in today before she goes on leave."

"Okay I'm going now. See you later, love you."

"Love you too, Jay, now get ya ass, we are leaving for the winery early in the morning," she replied before hanging up. I went to my closet, removing my uniform. instead opted for a distressed pair of shorts and a tan half shirt and paired it with my tan Yeezy slides.

"Where are you going dressed like that?"

"Nomi going on maternity leave, so I need my hair done. She can only fit me in today. You want to come, and we go out to eat afterwards?"

"I can't, babe. Ya'er is helping me get the rest of the things and then he is going to get his stuff for the trip. I'll see you tonight though," Nate said before kissing me on my lips and leaving out. I grabbed my purse and keys and went to my car. Blasting Latto, I pulled off to get my haired slayed. Vina's birthday was a special celebration, and we wanted to do our parts. When I pulled up and got inside, Nomi was waiting, and I was lowkey relieved because I didn't wait long. Four hours later, my hair was done along with my nails and toes. I was starving, so I pulled up to Uncaged Chefs and placed an order for the house. After getting home, I placed the food on the counter and saw Luka on the couch playing the game.

"Hey, Lil Bit."

"Hey, what you got going on?"

"Shit waiting on Nexus to decide if her ass going to cook or order food. What you about to do?"

"Eat, I bought Uncaged Chefs for everyone," I replied, knowing Nexus had enough on her plate.

"What you get."

"Jerk lamb chops, D'usse yams, Hennessy baked beans, mac and cheese with snickerdoodle banana pudding."

"Thanks, Lil Bit," Luka replied without looking up still playing his game. I hated when Nate played, he completely ignored me, and that shit pissed me off all the time.

"You want me to make your plate?"

"Nah you good. I will get up in a minute. There is a letter on the counter for you too."

After we talk for a minute, I went to open the letter and instantly, my body stiffened because I had an aunt asking me for money. How she knew where I was, I don't know, but I liked my life and not because of the stuff I had but because everyone here felt and treated me like family. Next year I'd be in college with my boyfriend and best friend so if paying my disruptive aunt to leave me alone was what was needed then so be it.

Jesscenda

When I was young, I used to read hood novels

and tell myself when things didn't go my way that girls like me don't give up but shit that's what I was doing. I was so hurt that my husband left me for my cousin that I convinced myself that a man who didn't want me was waiting for me. That's why I was sitting here with broken ribs, two black eyes, and a busted lip now. Juniece was right and yeah, I am shocked too that I said her name instead of calling her out of it. I was jealous for so long because she was everything I wasn't. With Davina, I treated her like my mother treated me like a meal ticket instead of my child and she didn't deserve that, but I can say I did right by her because I gave her to someone who always put her first and inspired her be more thana common nigga's wife to teach her envy can be your downfall and looks could be vain. I was not worthy of her, and I understood that many hours of sitting in that emergency room. New start where no one knows me was starting to sound better and better. Hopefully, my story had a better ending than being lonely who knows?

Luka

I watched Lil Bit's whole body stiffen. I knew what was wrong; the lady actually contacted us wanting us to pay for her not to come and take her away, but she had us completely fucked-up if she thought I was giving her crack head ass any type of money. She'd been living with us for a few months now and it felt like she truly belonged. I already knew that she had took money out of her account and gave her some money, but she didn't even have to do that; she was our family, we had her back so like a big brother, I was going to protect her. Something she never had until she met Nate and, US. My mother said she wanted to speak to me and already I knew it was going to be some good bullshit. One thing about Lee'Andra Musa, when she wanted to have her conversation, it was always bound to piss a nigga off. I hopped on a golf cart and drove right up to our house and the first thing I noticed that it was a car that I recognized all too well sitting in the driveway and prepared myself for the worst. My dad was a touchy subject because even though I knew he loved my mom; he also broke her. When we decided to not take anything he was offering, my mom cried for the first two straight years, putting on a brave face in front of me but when she thought I was sleep, she broke down. He was the love of her life.

"Ole lady where you at?" I called out. But she was far from that smooth, rich chocolate skin big dough ass, long hair, and still beautiful as if she was still in her twenties. Walking through the house, I was met with my pops staring me down and some basketball shorts and slides like he been working out. Even in his fifties, that nigga was buff as hell and even though we had our differences, I would never outright disrespect him.

"Son"

"Old man what you are doing here?" I joked. It wasn't no secret that him and my mom still saw each other from time to time. She was the love of his life; he just had a bad way of showing it.

"Just finished working out."

"Ma here? She said she wanted to talk to me about something."

"I wanted to talk to you. Son, I know the way I did your mom was wrong, and I take full responsibility for that. I hurt you both, and I realize my mistakes and even though your mom and I are working through our issues and building a relationship, I would also like to have a relationship with my son and would love for my kids to know their older brother." My father rambled the fact that him and my mother were back together news to me but to want me to build a relationship with his other kids wasn't happening.

"Long as you don't hurt my mom, I'm cool. As far as you and her, who am I to stop her happiness, but as far as getting to know your other kids hell no!" I yelled in anger.

"Ah ah you will not disrespect me. I get it you're mad but just like my blood runs through yours it runs through theirs, and I try to give you a choice but now I'm demanding. Rayden will be here in a few weeks, and you will not treat her like a stranger you understand me, son," my father said in his thick Nigerian accent. I had a whole bunch to say yet I said nothing. I can't remember Lil Bit and how we first had a conversation how she admitted that she wishes she had siblings to know then maybe life wouldn't have been so hard. It was true; I knew none of my siblings, but I knew all my father's wives and them bitches weren't worth a damn. The fact that he was fighting for my little sister's relationship with me, meant that she wanted it and as mad as I was, I guess I could do that for her. I just hope whichever kids showed up that they didn't bring their mother's personality and attitude with them cuz then I'd hurt her little ass feelings.

"Apologies, I meant no disrespect, baba. It's just it's easier to be mad than to realize how disappointed I was when you broke us and by your secrets."

"Son no one is perfect. We are all equally flawed, but this time you let go because how can you move forward holding on to the hate of the past. You're smart, successful, you don't need me for anything, but I want to be here to see my grandkids and be around this amazing family and village your mom and you created. I want us to be better, and I can only do that if you let me."

We sat quietly, letting the tension build. My father was right; I didn't want to be angry at him. I missed him, and a part of me was curious if any of his kids even looked like me. In the streets, I could be as vicious as I want to be but around family, I wanted to trust them to get me and in order to do that I had to learn to forgive and let the past go.

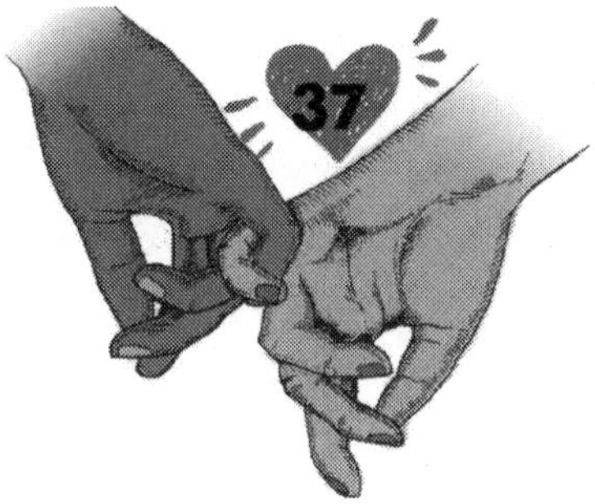

Juniece

The remodel for the winery was done, and everyone who mattered was here to celebrate Davina's ninth birthday, and she got her wish all of us dressed up as anime characters. Of course, we did fairytale characters. And Chance and Lyric chose one piece, and nobody love that anime we only like those two characters the rest of that shit was trash, so you know the whole party talked about it even the grandparents dressed up and when Demon came out, we all shared the moment finally that he was alive well and back to us. Word got back to us that Duke said he had unfinished business with Devin but truthfully, he couldn't compete. As much as I hated Jezebel, I know how much she truly loved him and the betrayal hopefully motivated her to do better because if she came back here, these hands was ready for everyone. Drita and Kano and KK chose reincarnated as a slime, and Nexus and her household came as Never Promised to Neverland and scared my damn daughter on her birthday. It took three candy bags four stories and a month worth of promises for her to go to sleep without any nightmares, so trust after this trip was over and we got back home, big bro going to have to see me. I watched from afar as my mom and Demon had their moment, and she cried while holding him and praying, and Santino came and sat next to me

"She missed him; you know?"

"Yeah, do so did I," I responded, thankful.

"Love come with lessons, mija, they prepare us for things we don't understand and things we fail to see. I'm not trying to be your dad, but I love your mom and I hope when I ask her to marry me you will support me"

"Papi chulo, you sure know I got you, but yeah it's been a long time since my mom was happy and you make her happy and you treat my kids like they're really your grandkids, so I got your back just don't make me regret it."

"I won't, mija. Davina, beneke," Santino scolded. When my journey started, who knew I would end up in love with my best friend and the mother to his kids? When he died, I thought big girls always the rider and never the one to have the happy ending, but he came back to me. He chose me and said the words I was waiting all my life to hear. He loved me.

EPILOGUE

Juniece

3 months later

I stood around the room thanking God for the family he allowed me to have. He brought Devin back into my life and every day, we were working to have our family. Jesscenda left with her kids, not looking back. I guess that ass whooping threw some sense into the ass. I wasn't better; what reason did I have to be. Yeah, she had Devin for a period in time, but I had them for life, and now I was pregnant with our third child. I didn't know what to do. Our family was growing and healing. Davina was doing great in school, and the bullying stopped but it didn't stop Ja'sai from making threats knowing her dad would get her out any trouble. He spoiled them kids, and I couldn't blame him. Devin missed out on so much to give our family and all that we had. As much as I wanted to say I was mad, I was thankful, for I had a second chance to love and all it took was for him to tell me he loved me. All my girls found a thug knight to their heart and hopefully, it stayed that way.

Nexus felt like even with all the love around her that the walls was constantly closing in and ended up higher in the new manager at the restaurant who was easy on her eyes and a smooth talker. Hopefully, she left it at that because if the lines get crossed, I hoped his mama had a black dress because Luka liked to kill way too much. He took pleasure in it, so she better speak now or forever hold her peace.

Devin

I never been so grateful in my life. I almost lost the love of my life making gambles, but it was her faith in me that allowed me to dream and give my family the life we have now. After being around Juicy, I fell for her deeper and deeper every day and spending time with kids was always a highlight for me. Like Kano promised, we bought the school, and my kids enjoyed the school life, but I'd been harassed to bullied which let me know I was doing everything right, but the way these little boys was looking at my daughters, I was going to shoot a few of them little niggas and that's okay. I was a work in progress but y'all be easy. Our story not over so just be patient with my girl, Tessa, she got some heat coming your way.

"Hey, what's up bro?" I asked, picking up.

"Hey, I'm about to get arrested for beating his niggas ass for being up in my wife's face. If I get arrested come and bail a nigga out."

"Luka, where you at?"

"The restaurant."

"Don't do shit. I'm on my way."

It was always something. No matter how hard stuff got, leaving was not an option, so I hope this knew what she was doing.

Drita

As I laid in the bed between my husband's legs. I allowed him to rub on my belly awaiting our son. I found myself still questioning why I was so lucky. See it don't matter where you come from, it matters how you show the beauty from your heart, and my husband taught me that. Every day, my kids motivated me to do better, and I wished my mother did the same for me. I still had yet to see her or hear from her and some days, I wished she was okay that she would show up clean sober and willing to love me without any limits. I talked to Mookie every now and then. He even came and seen the kids and even said he needed to talk to me about something important, which I didn't know what it could be, but he's always had my back and loved me e like a real dad, so I'd take what I can get and pray that God continue to look over my family and restore the things that damaged me.

Kano

Man, I loved my wife. She was beautiful and she loved the nigga down to my dirty drawers. I just hope she forgave me for the secret that I kept, and I hoped that she didn't leave me. I wasn't perfect. I made mistakes, but each day it goes without saying family over everything. With the new additions to our family, it was falling all into place. Chance and Lyric were still crazy as shit, and they welcomed two little boys and still ain't named them, so we just call them boy one and boy two damn shame but that's all I got. Just pray for the fam and when we come back, hope ain't nobody getting divorced.

Thank you for reading. Of course, this is not the ending for these couples because things were left unsaid. Unfortunately, they will have to wait until they speak to me. I have lost so many people. Mentally, I need to heal. Urban is draining, so I will try other genres to get my grove back. Please join my reading group Sis Are We Reading or Nah? for sneak peaks, visuals, and updates on my current works in progress.

Stay tuned for a sneak peak of my paranormal book that will drop 2023 this will be a standalone but before that, be introduced to the siblings.

Synopsis

Soul Renini had the world at her feet. Never had to think about the things in the outside world. Spoiled and materialistic, nothing mattered but the things she could buy until her parents forces her to marry a man she does not love.

Corvis Masters was never meant to exist. Labeled an outcast, he stayed to himself surrounded by his family. When trouble comes and Soul crosses his path, things take a turn for the worst.

When they choose each other, everyone makes objections? Fated lovers, will you choose to accept your fate or change your destiny?

Chapter 1: Goldie Masters

"Death is always around the corner. Live it like your last."

When I was child, a war took place between humans and fae world. Demons, vampires, wolves, Centaurs. A coup de tat took place throwing the world out of balance. Everybody wanted the power nobody wanted peace. No more of the old rules; they wanted the world to know who was more superior. The problem with power is it always attracts more power and problems. It was foretold that the humans were not ready to know of the world in the dark and powerful forces called the Hunters came in to put order in place. Hunters was skilled mixture of humans and fae, who knew of both world and served to keep the order. During that time, a prophecy was foretold of a centaur rare hybrid being born. Being that no one could foresee the parents of the and order to slaughter was sent out throughout the lands. The current rulers of the fae world lived for oppression and sent an order to kill my species off. Five thousand of my kind slaughtered and raped. My older sister, Gayla, hid me behind the wall in our living room and made me promise not to come out.

I watched them touch her and heard he screams and still she kept shaking her head, knowing I would run out at any moment. I couldn’t move at all when I came out, I held my sister and cried for her as if my soul itself left my body. Who knows how long I was there. In a time of desperation, a druid appeared and got me to safety in a land called Valitose. There I met another centaur. Being that we were the last of our kind, we married and Wenn became my husband. The first eight years was like the sweetest dream. But nothing lasts forever.

After our daughter, Fawllen, was born good days became far and between. Lands became barren and food became scarce, and murder became so normal that I feared for my family.

Knock, knock.

"With such blindness, how can you see?"

"Darkness is not what you should be afraid of for in the dark, I see clearly," I responded. The doors opened and there stood Sloane Baptist, a blind seer that can tell you your future and anything else you can imagine.

"Come in, Goldie. No need to explain, I understand my child. Grab the dragon bones and spread them out. You have suffered a great deal, and more is to come. In the coming of days, I see your death. If you run, they will kill your husband and your foal."

"How do I change my fate?" I said just above a whisper. But I did not get a reply. A lifetime of forever's was not meant for me. I watched my people slaughtered, so I could live and never understood why? I was supposed to survive to teach my husband how to love the woman who would bring in a new age of kings. And my daughter to nurture her brother as if he were mine. This is my fate that I had accept.

"What do I do?"

"You must send him and your daughter to the white forest there he must find the widowed pack queen, Zora. She will be at the spring on the north end with her children. She will be his new mate," she spoke as I gasp so loudly.

"Will she love my child the way I would?"

"No need to fear, for your sacrifice I will show you a glimpse of her future." Grabbing my head, a vision came. I saw my beautiful daughter with long red hair and golden, brownish eyes she inherited from me reading a book to this beautiful little boy, and it made me proud.

"Thank you."

"Goldie you daughter is eight, correct?"

"Yes," I replied as a man came from the back and handed me a jar.

"Give her this elixir and prepare her for the ceremony. This will be your only chance to unlock the powers you had sealed. She is centaur but a powerful witch as well and her destiny requires it for the war ahead," Sloane said as I came face-to-face with a man from my past.

"You are the man who saved me all those years ago. The druid."

"This is my husband, Clayton. I sent him to you years ago."

"I never got a chance to say this but thank you for what you did back then. If it wasn't for you, I would have died."

"It was nothing."

"It was more than you know. Will she be able to control her powers if I do?" I asked.

"The pack queen will nurture it."

"Sloan thank you," I said before leaving to head home. Like flicking a switch, my Centaur changing hitting the ground. I ran as my hair came blowing in the wind.

When I got home that evening, I watched my daughter ride on her father's back and laughing. When a centaur is born, the name given reflects the foal. Fawllen resembled both of us with her brown and white mane and slender frame. She truly was something beautiful. I knew that if I told Wenn what Sloane told me that he wouldn't excepted it. he would fight to the ends of the earth for the people he loves.

"Momma come play with us."

"What about dinner?"

"It's already done, my love. Now come play with us."

"How about we do change ceremony?"

"But Momma I'm scared. It will hurt," she said with tears streaming down her face.

"It's going to be okay, little one. You want to know why?

"Yes."

"When a centaur foal changes for the first time it's special. Do you know why we wait until a child turns eight before they can turn?"

"No, Momma."

"Well first we cleanse our bodies with impurities on our bodies and in our soul. Then, we learn our history, and then we accept the power given to us and saying the holy pledge. It is beautiful, and I will be there the whole time."

"Okay, Momma."

A bath was drawn of milk, herbs, lilies, and whole oranges. Once done, the altar was lit with black and white candles to represent the balance of the world. What you are deemed is what is in your heart.

"Momma, what if I am evil?"

"Papa and I will love you anyway but that is impossible because you're the kindest and sweetest child I know." It was very possible for a centaur to lean closer to evil, but my family always had a ritual done to avoid that very thing.

"Take a seat in the middle of the altar. We learn our history to understand who we are. It is said Centaurs are half-man, half-horse creatures that inhabited the mountains and forests of Thessaly. Centaurs were said to be primal, existing in tribes and making their homes in caves, hunting wild animals, and arming themselves with rocks and tree branches. There are many origin myths surrounding centaurs; one is that Centaurus, the offspring of King Ixion, mated with the cloud nymph, Nephele whom a jealous God Zeus created in the likeness of his wife Hera. They spawned centaurs and left them on Mount Pelion where the daughters of the immortal centaur Chiron nursed them.

Centaurs were followers of Dionysus, the God of wine and were thus known for being savage, rowdy, and boisterous. Often, they were portrayed as being governed by their bestial half.

Centaurs were creatures that represented chaos and barbarism, their likeness and proclivity for trouble were frequently described in Greek sculpture, myths, stories, and pottery. While boasting a bestial and lustful reputation, some centaurs only acted in such a way under the effects of wine and alcohol, which may have served as a cautionary tale. Being first generation hybrids saying the incantation inside of your heart will align you on the side of good or evil.

During the early stages of war, a Centaur Brynzin fell in love with witch Kalinda and they had an offspring hybrid Rhynna. We are descendants of Rhynna, through your beast feel the earth between your toes. Align your mental state with the wind. Drink this through Kalinda find your passion to fight and like water flow through your body as if it's one. Do you feel it."

"Yes."

"Say the incantation meant for you."

"I Fawllen Masters, pledge to stand on everything the light touches and defend the balance of world. I am a beast of nature. I am elements of Gods. I am one," Fawllen spoke. Turning like the swift wind into a foal stumbling to walk for the first time.

"Slowly."

"Look Papa, I'm walking."

“I see, but it’s time to eat. Until you can do it on your own say enchant to turn back into my beautiful daughter.”

“Yes, Daddy. Enchant.”

Sitting around the table I enjoyed the conversation between my family. Fawllen had a big personality telling me all about her day and how her dad was showing her how to hunt and how they missed me. I warmed my heart that she at least had one of us.

Placing her in her bed, I kissed her forehead and went to my room. When I got in the room when was laying in the bed waiting for me. I laid in his chest, trying to remember his scent all while discussing the white forest as much as wanted to hide the truth I ended up telling Wenn anyway. At first, he resisted and then I told him what he needed to hear. After crying we made love one final time.

The morning came and it was bittersweet. I knew I would never see my sweet daughter or loving husband again. Although it was necessary doesn't mean it didn't hurt any less.

"By momma, don't cry we'll see you later," Fawllen said, wiping the tears that fell.

"No, sweetheart not this time. Remember I love you more than anyone in my world and understand no matter what happen, I am with you." I hugged her tight as I could, kissing her forehead.

"You protect her Wenn with all of your being and know that I love you more than time itself."

"And I you. We can fight this together. We can find a way. How can you ask me to love another when you are it for me?" When spoke kissing me with his soft full lips between words.

"Wenn this is so hard my love, even now I am breaking speaking these words and still I will rather die knowing that you and my daughter will help save the world, instead we all die. Please. Go and don't look back. We don't have much time!" I yelled with tears falling. I placed Fawllen on her father's back.

"Fawllen, you hold on to Papa and you promise me you won't look back. Be a big girl."

"I will Momma, I love you."

"And I you my precious one. Go!" I yelled, watching my husband ride, and hearing my child scream for me. Changing, I grabbed my sword riding to meet the fight allowing Wenn and Fawllen to escape. When I got into town, bodies filled the grounds; men, women, and children died.

"There she is. Capture her," the demon known as Silas called out.

"You will die," I said, running to kill Silas for murdering my sister, but before I reached him...

Made in the USA
Middletown, DE
19 July 2022

69690511R00172